PRINCE & PIRATE

ELLIOT COOPER

© 2018 Elliot Cooper

All rights reserved. This book is a work of fiction. This book or any portion thereof may not be reproduced or used in any manner whatsoever without the express written permission of the publisher except for the use of brief quotations in a book review.

Cover Art: Elliot Cooper

Author's Notes: This story was originally published in 2016 and this version contains no additional content.

Content Warning: Contains sexual content, capture fantasy elements, mental illness slurs, a sadistic narcissistic villain, and a parent with undiagnosed frontotemporal dementia in a low fantasy setting.

PRINCE & PIRATE

Content Warning: Contains sexual content, capture fantasy elements, mental illness slurs, a sadistic narcissistic villain, and a parent with undiagnosed frontotemporal dementia in a low fantasy setting.

Prince Gavin is powerless to refuse when his father demands he secure an alliance with a distant kingdom. At first, he sees the journey as a chance to prove his worth and indulge in the grand adventures of his dreams. Yet nothing seems right about his father's paranoid insistence he travel by merchant ship while disguised as a diplomat. Once out on the open sea, Gavin learns he's been tricked into boarding an infamous pirate ship: the *Ebon Drake*.

Captain Marcas Drake is delighted to discover the courtier he's kidnapped is really a prince. Acquiring such a hefty ransom will prove once and for all he's a brilliant pirate in his own right, not riding the coattails of his father's fame. And using his charms to seduce his prisoner makes for an entertaining pastime. But unfortunate events turn the Ebon

Drake's crew against their captain before the ransom can be carried out.

Marooned, Marcas and Gavin's new equal footing turns the pirate's sensual game into something else entirely. However, being stranded on a tiny island becomes the least of their worries when rescue arrives in the form of the bloodthirsty Crimson Queen, a pirate who's been chasing Marcas for years. Working together to escape the queen is their only hope of freedom and a chance their growing love might outlast their misadventures.

For Shawn, who waited nine years for this story to be completed.

Thank you, Mooselings, for your encouragement.

CHAPTER 1

"I'M SENDING YOU TO HIGHBRON—ALONE," KING MALCOLM said. His stony expression revealed more than his tone; he would not back down.

Prince Gavin's chest tightened, understanding he needed no further proof of his father's loosening grip on reality. Send his sole male heir across the sea to a foreign land alone? No sane king would order such a thing.

His father had been losing touch with the world at large over the past five years. It had been disheartening to watch the once warm, tactically minded man become paranoid about traitors, spies, and the threat of pirates to their island townships sprinkled throughout the expanse of Siren's Deep. But the ridicule he levelled at his son for the imagined slight of not being Malcolm's exact copy ripped Gavin's emotions to tatters. Gavin clung to a sliver of affection for his father, yet it was difficult to tell if the man could remember he once shared that tender emotion.

"You won't send any guards with me? They're not mere travelling companions, Father," Gavin said. Once the words were out of his mouth, he regretted their lecturing slant.

"I know what they are, boy." The king's nostrils flared in annoyance as his voice rose. "You *will* be travelling alone. In disguise. Make your preparations for your personal belongings. You leave at midnight."

Gavin's brows furrowed. Why so much caution, only to throw him to the wolves once he was away from the safety of Castle Crakesyde? And why the sudden rush? His father had first mentioned his plan in a vague sense a week before, declaring it again at dinner that evening. Surely a week wasn't enough time to make all the necessary arrangements.

"Am I to travel on a navy ship?" It wasn't as though Gavin hated travel or the idea of getting out and seeing the world. In fact, he was rather enamoured of the concept. A trip on one of Crakesyde's navy vessels would ensure his personal safety and allow him to experience the world in a way he hadn't been afforded in his eighteen years. But all hopes were dashed when his father frowned. He knew that look: intense disgust wrapped in consternation.

"You'd have an entire entourage of navy vessels parade you across Siren's Deep, wouldn't you, boy? And what purpose would that serve?" The king stared hard at Gavin for a moment and barrelled on as soon as he opened his mouth to reply. "It would draw undue attention! You'd be a beacon for cutthroats! All that roiling of the sea would draw the creatures from the depths! Leviathans! Sea dragons! Sharks! Besides, the royal navy isn't a chauffeur or well-dressed nanny; those men do real work!"

"I didn't mean more than one ship, Father," Gavin protested. His pale face flushed red in embarrassment. The king might not think anything of calling his son a fool within earshot of the guards outside his chamber door, but Gavin knew the power of perception. He would never be able to gain the respect of the castle's staff if they all thought him incompetent and thoughtless based on the king's frequent vocal assumptions. "I understand the importance of the Royal Navy keeping the plague of pirates in check."

"Then you should also understand that just last week two of our navy vessels were destroyed by this 'plague.' All because my so-called advisors on the King's Council felt I should send patrols away from our coastal border. The fools!" King Malcolm's fist slammed down on the ornate table beside his chair. He didn't look moved by the shock on Gavin's face. "Two separate incidences, both within our nearest colonies. The Crimson Queen, that wretched wench! She went on to sack the township of New Auchen! The gall!"

"A-and the other incident?"

"Who do you think? That blasted Captain Drake! At least he left the nearest township alone. But that's saying nothing for the fine sailors we lost." With that thought weighing heavily in the king's private sitting room, Malcolm closed his eyes for a moment and rubbed his temples. When he looked at his son again, he pointed a thin finger. "You will be my diplomat *only*, do you understand? You will travel as other courtiers do, by merchant ship. I have secured passage for you on the *Maiden Fair*, which is due in port in a fortnight. You will travel by coach to Crowsmouth. This is an order from your father and king, and I will not hear any further protests! These precautions are all for your own safety and the continued safety of our sailors. I wish you to succeed in your mission as we've discussed and return with good news."

"Should I speak with anyone on the Council regarding arrangements?" Gavin set his teeth to keep from saying anything more to inflame his father's ire.

"You should speak with no one about the nature of your journey. The less outsider involvement, the better. I've made the arrangements for your travel myself—an added precaution against my detractors." Malcolm's anger cooled as he settled back down into his favourite chair beside the large empty hearth.

Gavin nodded his understanding of his father's instructions. What the king wanted, he was entitled to. If he wanted to send his son on a suicide mission, so be it.

"I will make haste, My King," Gavin said, returning to old formalities. He bowed, turned, and strode out of the king's chambers with what little dignity he had left.

His mind buzzed with hypothetical situations as he headed down the curving corridors towards the east wing. For once in his life, he ignored the grand paintings of pastoral scenes, griffins, knights vanquishing dragons, and ancestral portraits. What if the merchant ship was attacked by pirates? What if his identity was discovered? There was even the possibility he would never make it to Crowsmouth, what with bandits and wild beasts on the road and riverways. And there was the added worry the crown prince of Highbron was a wretch Gavin wouldn't dream of asking to marry his sister.

Then, as if he'd summoned her by thought alone, Effie darted out of the library down the hall. Her golden gown rustled, and her bright-red hair began to fall out of its dainty bun as she ran to meet him.

"I heard your footsteps and couldn't wait. What did he say?" She bounced on the balls of her slippered feet.

"I'm to visit Prince Redmond and arrange your marriage, just as the king announced at dinner," Gavin said, tone stiff.

"Don't act so affronted, Gav. You've always talked about travelling, seeing the world with your own eyes." Effie's rolled skyward. "Did you fight again? You only call Father that when he's in one of his moods."

"He's always in 'one of his moods' when I'm around." Gavin frowned. He tried to pinpoint the moment, the month, the day his father had forgot how to be anything but irritated with him. A party the previous spring came to mind. "Ever since that incident with Duke Waldren."

"Father said he doesn't care about that—"

"So long as it doesn't interfere with my marriage prospects," Gavin finished for her. He shook his head and walked on towards the library. He couldn't help his proclivities any more than his father could help his ever-increasing paranoia, it seemed. And while no one would bat an eye at Gavin's interest in men, he had the responsibility of producing heirs and, therefore, a need to acquire a queen.

"You're not getting off the hook that easily!" Effie caught up and walked next to him, hooking her arm with his. "That's an old, dead battle. What's really the matter? You're not afraid of travelling by ship, are you? I know you can swim."

Gavin shook his head as he steered his sister through the open ornate-wood doors and into the library. "He's not sending any bodyguards with me. In fact, it's our father's royal decree that I travel alone."

"His what?!" Effie's arm slipped from Gavin's. She narrowed her eyes, hands on her hips. "You march back in there and tell him you'll do no such thing! Assert your princely right! Remind him you're his only heir!"

Gavin sat down in the nearest cushioned chair and picked up a book lying on the small table beside it. *A Highbronian History: Volume One* was familiar. It covered the founding of Highbron on the once-barren rock pile of a continent to the northwest, where Crakesyde had beat Anthea in a race to discover new, uninhabited islands to colonise. It had flourished as the largest Crakesydian colony for centuries until its governing Duke had declared her people's independence. Effie must have been reading about the kingdom that would likely be her future home.

He opened the book and pretended to read the words printed on the pages, but the lines ran together. His mind was consumed with his impending voyage, and he already knew the first volume was rather boring and written from a biased Crakesydian viewpoint. The feud between the two nations had fizzled to mere gruffness with time, but a marriage of royal bloodlines would go a long way to show Crakesydian and Highbronian people alike that the old grudge had at last been buried.

"I can't go against his orders, Effie, and you know it," he said with a sigh. He shut the book and placed it back on the table gingerly. "Father wants me to lie low, pretend to be a diplomat, and make it back in one piece."

"He asks too much," Effie said in a huff. She crossed her arms over her chest. "Why not send a real diplomat, a real courtier?"

"If I pretend to know our father at all, I'd wager he has high hopes that such an experience will force me to be a 'real man' and focus on the worries of a king, not a patron of the arts."

"Only if you aren't robbed and murdered before you ever make it to Highbron." Effie bit her lip. Tears welled in her eyes, and she turned away from him as she walked over to the large windows overlooking the courtyard's elaborate gardens.

"Would you mind helping me pack?"

Effie shook her head slowly but didn't move away from the window until he rose from his chair. She turned to face him and then rushed at him, throwing her arms around him.

"You'll want to take half the library if I don't help you," she said between quiet sniffles.

∽

"You look fine, sire," the chauffer sitting opposite Gavin

said, but his worried expression told Gavin he thought otherwise. "Every bit the diplomat."

Gavin stepped out of the coach and looked around the docks. He tried to take in the sights, sounds, and repugnant smells all at once. The people bustling to and fro, getting the day's work started amazed him. He'd visited the heart of the city of Crowsmouth once as a child, but he hadn't been allowed near the docks. It was too dangerous, his father had said, and he'd stayed at the large family estate overlooking Auchen Bay.

But this was the living breathing heart of the city, and Gavin felt out of place. His clothing seemed awkward, and the feathered hat he wore was absurdly flamboyant. He regretted letting his sister dress him in the latest fashion. The clothes, done in rich greens and gold, were supposed to make him look like a baron's son, but he felt like a brocaded peacock.

Heads turned as his footmen unloaded his twin trunks from the coach. He watched, using them as a visual distraction to ease his frazzled nerves. How was he supposed to go unnoticed with such an entourage? Perhaps his father was having him over, a final cruel joke before he left the kingdom. But Gavin knew that wasn't his father's style. The king was many things, but he wasn't a practical joker.

"You're certain this is the normal attire of a royal diplomat? I've never felt so ridiculous in my life," Gavin said to his chauffer as the other man exited the coach.

"The king really keeps you in the dark, doesn't he, Your Hi—er, sir?" The chauffer nearly slipped yet again. He'd been placed under strict orders from the king and the prince to regard him as 'sir' or 'sire' in public.

"Yes, regarding certain official business concerns. Such as the current attire of diplomats," Gavin replied with caution. He thought it best to leave out his true thoughts. It was common knowledge to many of the castle's serving staff that the king kept many things from the prince, only to berate him later for not knowing anything about national policy. He hoped, for his own sake, the staff saw the king's contradictions for what they were.

"It's the latest, sire. Stuffy, but fashionable." The chauffer nodded before directing the footmen for a moment. Then he turned and handed a thick envelope with a broken seal to Gavin. "These're your travelling papers. Make sure you present them to the captain of the *Maiden Fair* when you board or else he might think you're pulling his leg."

Gavin turned the envelope over in his hands. It was really happening. He was going to see distant lands, take an ocean voyage, and have a chance to prove to his father that he was worthy of inheriting the throne. He took a deep breath and smiled at the chauffer. All visions of his sister's tear-streaked face as she said goodbye the night before were shoved to the back of his mind. He would see her again.

"You're certain there's nothing I could say or do that would give you cause to join me on board?"

"'Fraid not, sire. I get seasick and there's only passage booked for one as it stands." The chauffer flashed a grim smile at Gavin. "Please take care of yourself, sir."

"Thank you." Gavin nodded in farewell and followed after the footmen towards one of the closer piers.

There were many different types of sailing ships docked in Auchen Bay or anchored farther out in the expansive inlet: small schooners built for speed, cargo ships in various sizes, and the grand warships of the Royal Navy. According to his father, the *Maiden Fair* was an older three-mast cargo ship. Gavin scanned the larger vessels, trying to spot the right name.

If he'd known about the trip at least a week in advance, he could have done proper research on sailing ships. He had minimal knowledge of life at sea, which was sure to make him that much more of an outsider to the *Maiden*'s crew. His father had told him, at least, that the crew would typically keep to themselves so long as he didn't get in their way. Seafaring men had little respect for people ignorant to their ways and the hardships faced on the open ocean, but they weren't likely to go out of their way to bother a paying passenger. Gavin knew his father had earned some experience in the navy when he'd been Gavin's age. He tried not to think the man had kept anything important from him.

"There it is." The footman's loud voice jarred Gavin out of his thoughts.

"That? I'm going across the sea in *that*?" Gavin's voice caught in his throat. He swallowed hard as he looked at the large merchant ship ahead of them. It was old and dark. Very old, from what he could tell. The thing barely looked seaworthy. It must have seen more pirate attacks and foul winds than every other ship in the harbour combined. He blinked twice at some strange markings on the battered side. "Are those... Aren't those the sort of marks made by giant squid?"

"I wouldn't know, sir," the closer footman replied. His eyes seemed riveted to the trunk he carried.

Gavin ignored the apparent state of the ship for the moment. He was no expert on how to keep a vessel afloat. Obviously she floated well enough at the side of the pier. But as they drew closer to the *Maiden Fair*, it became more apparent the ship didn't live up to its name in the least.

Yet he couldn't keep a wry smile from quirking up the corners of his lips. He'd dreamed of having a grand adventure for most of his life, had devoured every book he could find on famous pirates and the sailors who hunted them, both fact and fiction. Now, he'd get a sea adventure of his very own, whether he was ready for it or not.

Before he could ask his ill-informed footmen any more

questions, they deposited his trunks at the base of a gangplank. The taller of the two hailed one of the sailors and began to explain the trunks were for the *Maiden*'s new passenger.

"That fellow there?" The sailor coughed in a poor attempt to hide her laugh. She nodded to Gavin, who'd walked up to stand beside his belongings. The old woman grinned with disgusting teeth, some of which were missing. "Aye, I'll be fetchin' the captain for ye. Wait here, lads."

The footmen exchanged nervous glances. Gavin didn't like the look of the sailor either, but he wasn't about to pass judgment on someone who'd lived a hard life. Not everyone was lucky enough to be born into privilege. It didn't take much time in the library to figure that out, sheltered as he might have been from the daily lives of those not born into power or wealth.

"Sire?" the taller footman asked quietly. "Will you be needing us for anything else?"

Gavin swallowed hard and cleared his throat. The comfort of having people near him who knew who he was would be over soon enough anyway. There was no reason to keep the footmen in an uncomfortable situation any longer than they had to be. He gestured back towards the waiting coach.

"Have a safe journey back to Auchencrow," he said and forced a small smile.

The footmen breathed sighs of relief, said their farewells, and then hurried off.

Alone with his trunks and travelling papers, Gavin glanced up the gangplank and saw a few sailors milling about on the deck. Most of them looked like they'd spent decades at sea, and a good portion of them sported greying or white hair. It didn't inspire fresh confidence regarding the competence of the ship. *At this rate*, he thought cynically, *the captain will be as old as my father and just as sane.*

Then, a handsome sailor, who looked to be well into his thirties, sauntered down the gangplank. His neatly trimmed black goatee and bright eyes caught Gavin's attention first; then his gaze shifted over the sailor's strong shoulders and arms, down to his outstretched hand.

"You must be Mr. Reginald Smith." The sailor's broad grin showed confidence and much better oral hygiene than the other members of the *Maiden*'s crew.

Unused to being Mr. Smith, Gavin shook off the quizzical look on his face and handed over the envelope. "Yes, I'm Mr. Smith. And these are my travelling papers."

"Yes, of course." The sailor extracted the various papers from the envelope and looked them over. His thick brows rose—in surprise or approval, it was hard to tell—and he turned back to the ship. "Mr. Dawkins! Have someone bring Mr. Smith's luggage on board, if you please!"

The orders struck Gavin as strange at first. Then it hit him as quite obvious: the man tucking his travelling papers into his pocket was the captain of the ship. The *Maiden Fair* certainly had an odd crew.

"Now, Mr. Smith, if you'll follow me, please," the captain said and gestured for Gavin to follow him onto the ship. "I'm Captain MacLeod, and I'll have you know I run a tight ship. Everyone knows their place on board, their duties, and I expect you to do the same. I understand you're used to being in a position of authority, but now that you've set foot on my ship, you'll respect my authority as captain. And while I'm aware you've paid in advance to be our passenger, I won't have you disrupting my crew."

"I understand," Gavin said with a nod. He tried to take in all the happenings on deck, but there was too much going on to tear his focus away from the captain. The man's confidence put him at ease. He didn't feel, for the time being at least, that the ship was doomed to sink as soon as she hit open water. It wouldn't hurt to have the handsome captain to chat with on the long journey either. "I was told the voyage would take four weeks?"

"That's a rough estimate, but given fair winds, it shouldn't take much more than that. Have you ever been to Highbron before?" The captain opened a door that led to a spacious cabin.

Gavin stepped across the threshold and saw the captain had comfortable tastes. The decor was eclectic, with items from at least five different cultures he recognised. A large round wooden table burnished with Anthean sigils dominated one side of the cabin, while the other side featured an intimate sitting area and an embroidered Naavetian curtain separating a sleeping space. The furniture was worn, stained in places, but still gave the impression of understated wealth. Or, perhaps, diminishing wealth. It couldn't have been easy to maintain any sort of business with the dramatic increase in pirate activities over the past five years.

"I've never left Crakesyde before," Gavin admitted. There was no reason to hide that sort of information. He was already lying about who he was, no need to lie about anything else if he could help it. The captain was an honest merchant just going about his business. Gavin felt rather ashamed at his forced charade, but showed no outward signs of it. "I've always wanted to, though I'm hoping for an uneventful journey."

The captain chuckled.

"The sea is unpredictable, Mr. Smith. I can only make you hollow promises about the likelihood of an easy voyage." He sat down in the most prominent chair in the cabin, which was upholstered in balding burgundy velvet. The clawed yet simple wooden legs were distinctly Highbronian in style.

"Have a seat. Please, make yourself comfortable. The crew will be loading supplies for at least another hour."

Gavin sat in the chair across from the captain and pretended his rear wasn't sinking oddly into the cushion's middle. He smiled thinly, unsure of what to say next. It was his turn to speak, and in the rules of polite society, it was his duty to carry on the conversation.

"I hope you've brought more practical clothing with you," the captain said with a crooked smirk. He made no attempt to hide his almost leering appraisal of Gavin as he shrugged leisurely and slouched into a more comfortable repose. "It might be best to dress as a more common man, if you can bring yourself to do it. In case of pirate attacks, of course. They're likely to single out anyone who doesn't fit in. Especially someone dressed as magnificently as yourself, Mr. Smith."

"I…didn't bring any plain clothes," Gavin stammered. His eyes narrowed at the captain. He wasn't sure whether or not to be offended by his implication that he would be loath to "lower" himself by wearing clothes not of his station. His cheeks flushed. It was certainly embarrassing to not have thought to bring along clothes that would suit a long sea voyage. But it would have been more embarrassing to admit that most of the clothing for this trip had been chosen by his sister and valet.

A loud noise and a series of shouts broke through the tension accumulating in the room. The captain sprang to his feet and dashed out of the cabin. Gavin followed close behind and lost his hat as a gust of wind greeted him. He wasn't worried about recovering the dreadful thing, catching the attention of the nearest sailor instead.

"Was that a splash I heard?"

"Aye! Young Morris lost 'is footing again. Dead clumsy 'e is!" The grizzled old sailor laughed.

Gavin watched the commotion at the gangplank. The captain shouted orders. Barrels were strewn about on deck, down the gangplank, and on the dock below. Crew members rushed to gather the barrels.

"Isn't someone going to help him out of the water?" Gavin noticed no one had moved to assist Morris.

"We ain't nannies. 'E's a sailor, same's the rest of us. An' if 'e can't swim by now 'e's got no business bein' 'ere." With that comment, the old sailor turned to look at Gavin properly. He sucked in a sharp breath, and his eyes went wide, as if he'd seen a ghost.

"What is it?"

"Captain! You've doomed us all to the depths!" the sailor shouted over the din. He pointed at Gavin and flailed his brown hand to garner as much attention as possible. "Look 'ere!"

Again, it was time for Gavin's face to flush deep pink.

"What is it, Broderick?" the captain called back from across the deck.

"It's a redhead, Captain! You're expectin' us to set sail with a redhead on board?" Broderick spluttered. He took two steps back from Gavin, as if his hair colour might be catching.

The captain glared at the sailors staring at Gavin, unfazed by the older man's dramatics. "Back to work! All of you! I'm not about to let some silly superstition run my ship!"

Gavin frowned at the captain as he approached, but he was glad Broderick sprinted off across the deck to get back to his duties.

"You'll have to excuse my crew. We've been at sea for practically four months straight, and they're a little jumpy." The captain smiled at Gavin apologetically.

Gavin nodded. He imagined being stuck in the same

space for weeks and months on end would make anyone a little stir crazy.

He'd heard the old superstitions about sailing before. Redheads were bad luck. Two redheads on board meant certain doom for the ship. Sea birds and sea creatures brought bad luck to anyone who harmed them. There were countless more bad omens for sailors, but he was only aware of the most prevalent ones.

"Being jumpy is entirely understandable," Gavin said, returning the captain's smile.

"Follow me; I'll show you to your cabin." The captain walked off towards the middle of the ship and headed below deck without waiting to see if Gavin would follow.

CHAPTER 2

THE SUN AT HIS BACK, CAPTAIN MARCAS DRAKE STARED OUT over the deep blue water still tinged with gold from the recent sunrise. Siren's Deep, the largest sea in the northern hemisphere, was his most beloved playground.

He felt much more comfortable with his cutlass at his side and both pistols strapped across his chest. Having tucked away the more respectable garb of a merchant for use in a future ruse, he'd donned his usual clothing, half obscured by the stately black and gold long coat that had become as much a trademark as his name.

The plan had been to wait until they were two days out before removing the false name from the stern of the ship. Two days until they could all don their weapons again and forget about not mentioning the name Drake. But Marcas could tell his crew was restless and, after the first night, allowed everything to fall back to normal.

When King Malcolm's diplomat awoke, he'd have quite the surprise: kidnapped by one of the most infamous pirates alive! And all the idiot had thought to bring along were two trunks full of fancy clothes, books, two small portraits of a redheaded girl, and a rapier. He counted himself lucky the man hadn't become seasick as soon as they'd left Crowsmouth. Clearly Mr. Smith had spent too much time among lordlings and not enough in the real world.

"Captain Drake, the crew wants to know if they can toss the prisoner's lady portraits overboard. You know how they are," Mr. Dawkins, the quartermaster, said in a low voice. He took his battered tricorn hat off and ran a hand through his prematurely grey hair. With the hat over his heart, he followed his captain's gaze out over the water. "Can't say I blame 'em really. They give me the chills just knowing we've got 'em on board with Smith bein' a redhead himself. It's like there's three of 'em."

"You know how I feel about superstitions, Mr. Dawkins," Marcas said with a wry grin. "I'll keep them in my cabin, and you can tell the men they've been drowned if they're all that bothered by some paint on canvas."

"Thank you, sir," Mr. Dawkins said with an uneasy smile. He put his hat back on and turned to make his way down the stairs to the main deck.

"And Mr. Dawkins," Marcas said before the quartermaster was out of earshot. "Have Mr. Smith join me for breakfast. Tie his hands if he makes any threats or struggles."

"Aye, aye, Captain Drake," Mr. Dawkins replied before marching down the stairs to the main deck.

"You're to have breakfast with the captain. Or else," Mr. Dawkins barked after banging on the door.

Gavin, blinking with confusion at the rude awakening, couldn't protest when Mr. Dawkins wrenched open the door and shoved a pistol in his face.

"You don't have to behave like a brigand, sir," Gavin said,

his tone curt. He didn't understand why the man hadn't simply asked him to report to the captain's cabin. What had happened while he'd slept? Hadn't he been cordial with Captain MacLeod?

"Five minutes. Get dressed. I'll be right outside. Don't try anything funny." Mr. Dawkins sneered at Gavin before exiting the small cabin in a huff.

Under the pretence of finding the right outfit for the occasion, Gavin dug through his larger trunk in an attempt to find his rapier. It wasn't his favourite blade, but it was well made. He swallowed a mild wave of panic when he discovered the weapon wasn't there. Heart thudding rapidly, he pressed onward. There was no other choice. Luckily, he found his sister had possessed the forethought to pack him two sets of plainclothes after all, though she'd buried them in the bottom of the trunk. He'd still be an obvious outsider on the ship, but it would have to do.

Before Gavin could lament the loss of his only source of protection, Mr. Dawkins burst back into the room.

"C'mon. Mustn't keep the captain waiting any longer," the sailor said gruffly. He waved his pistol about some more.

Gavin sighed and allowed himself to be led to the captain's cabin. He noticed as they crossed the main deck that no one paid them any mind. None of the crew seemed to find it odd their quartermaster was treating their passenger in such a way. He would inform the captain it was unnecessary to force Gavin to attend meals with him.

Mr. Dawkins knocked once on the captain's cabin door. A shout from the other side of the door his cue to open it, Dawkins shoved him inside.

Gavin steadied himself with a hand pressed against the doorframe and looked up to see the captain seated at the far end of his large table. The captain, now dressed in a handsome long coat instead of drab brown work clothes, poured a dark liquid into two goblets.

"Good morning, Mr. Smith. I trust you slept well?" The captain gestured for Gavin to join him at the table where a place had already been set for him.

Gavin seated himself but didn't return the captain's pleasantries.

"Your quartermaster has the most appalling manners. I can only hope you didn't order him to treat me, a passenger whose place on board was secured with gold, like some sort of prisoner." Gavin tried to keep his expression as neutral as possible.

"Oh, he didn't tell you?" The captain smirked at Gavin's indignant attitude. "You *are* some sort of prisoner. My prisoner, in fact."

"Excuse me?" Gavin's mouth clamped shut in shock. Had everyone gone mad over the course of one night?

"Forgive me for not introducing myself properly yesterday." He reached over the table and placed one of the goblets near Gavin's plate. "I'm Captain Marcas Drake."

Gavin stopped breathing for a moment. Just like that, he was proven right about his father's hare-brained scheme. Only he wished the old man had been right instead. He wished he hadn't needed to book passage on a navy ship just to ensure his own safety. But that was all pointless to think about now. Captain Drake, one of the most well-known pirates of the age, had him trapped.

The state of the ship made sense now. It *was* a very old ship and had seen plenty of battles. Everyone knew Captain Drake had inherited his ship from his father, Deadeye Angus Drake, the most feared pirate in recorded history. And with the realisation that he was actually on board the *Ebon Drake* herself, a ship mired in the most daring and inglorious side of history, Gavin's fear turned to nervous excitement.

"This is the *Ebon Drake?*" His eyes went wide.

"Yes." Captain Drake chuckled. He gestured to the food set out on the table and then served himself some eggs, ham, and sliced apples. "Don't forget to help yourself to breakfast. I won't have you starving yourself."

Gavin blinked and went about putting some food on his plate. He wasn't hungry, but knowing the true nature of his situation, he thought it best to eat anyway. There was no telling when they'd feed him next.

"What happened to the *Maiden Fair*? Is it even a real ship?" Gavin asked, but the look in Captain Drake's eyes made him wish he could take the questions back.

"She was a real ship. We intercepted her a few weeks back and found some interesting items in the captain's log." Captain Drake shrugged. "An opportunity we couldn't pass up."

"Weeks?" Gavin's face fell. That meant his father had been planning this ordeal for months. His father didn't trust him at all, despite the nature of his mission. But what if the mission itself was a farce? What if his father expected him to fail and sent him instead of some trusted courtier for just that reason? He shook his head. How could he think of his own problems when Captain Drake had just admitted to destroying the real *Maiden Fair*? "It *was* a real ship?"

"We didn't kill the crew if that's what you're worried about," Captain Drake said around a mouthful of food.

∼

"We don't know nothin', Y-yer Majesty!" the sailor bleated. Tears leaked out of his eyes in continuous streams, washing thin lines of dirt off his grimy forehead. He squirmed a little in fear, but the rope lashing his ankles to the bend of a large palm tree held fast. A glance sideways at his two companions, strung up alongside him, added to his visible distress.

"I want to believe you; really, I do." The dark-haired pirate let out a light, patronising laugh. She pressed the edge of her sword against the man's throat, gesturing to the other men dangling beside him. "Your shipmates want me to believe you! Because if I don't? Why now, I'd have to slit your lying throat, my dear Captain."

"We was ambushed," one of the others shouted weakly. "They broadsided us!"

"We lost our bearings!" the third cried.

The woman rolled her right eye. She walked down the line and grabbed the third sailor by the hair, jerking his head to the side so that he could look at her more properly. His eyes fixed on the diamond and ruby studded skull and crossbones of her eye patch. Without warning, his face scrunched up into an ugly, wrinkled mess, and he blubbered like a baby.

"Hush, hush," she said soothingly, lips pursed. Her tone remained calm, but the emotion she let him see in her green eye was that of pure cruelty. "Tell your queen everything, dearie. Tell her which way Captain Drake sailed. Tell her if he was planning anything delightfully nefarious."

Snot trickled out of the sailor's nostrils as he tried, in vain, to control his emotions. He sniffed sharply and let out a ragged breath before speaking, tearing his eyes from the pirate's eye patch. "H-how do you kn-know it was Drake?"

"Because he's so miserably predictable!" she screeched in the man's face. It only succeeded in making him sob anew, so she let his head drop. "I hope you're drowned in your own spittle you bilge-swilling coward!"

"Please, Yer 'ighness…it 'ad to be some easterly bearing. On my 'onour," the middle sailor said in a pleading voice.

That made her grin in delight, showing her yellowed

teeth to the men. She pinched the middle man's cheek as if he were a child who had just done something adorable.

"Good boy!" This time she outstretched her sword so the blade pressed again to their captain's throat. "How long ago did he strand you here? I'd gamble two weeks at least by how awful you lot smell. Imagine, sailors afraid of water!"

Her shrill laugh made the sailors cringe, but the interrogation was interrupted by one of the pirate's own crew members.

A tall, wiry, dark-brown man wearing little but faded red breeches and a leather vest approached. He gave the sailors a discerning glance before addressing his captain. "By your leave, My Queen. The rest refused service."

"Refused service to the Crimson Queen?" the pirate captain said through clenched teeth. "I'll kill them all, Arreid!"

"No, you must'n't! Please have pity. Have mercy!" the merchant captain begged.

"Belay your tongue, fool! I've had enough of your unhelpful whinging!" the Crimson Queen shouted.

The sailor whimpered.

With a sharp jerk of her arm, she slashed the man's throat open, her lip curled in agitation.

The other two sailors shouted in fear as the blood gushed from their captain's neck and flowed out onto the sand below. The queen wiped her blade off on the third sailor's shirt as he passed out.

"Arreid? Did you find anything of interest on the *Maiden Fair*?" she asked as they walked away from the sobbing and shouting man still dangling from the palm tree. She sheathed her sword for the time being. Sea air wasn't good for the blade after all.

"The captain's log and all food supplies were missing, My Queen," Arreid said.

"And the rum?"

"Not a drop on board." He gave her a wry smile.

"I'm surprised the crowing bastard didn't carve his name in the foremast."

CHAPTER 3

Two weeks crept by and Marcas felt tensions on board growing. The crew were increasingly restless, and he could hear plenty of grumblings about not being able to do as they pleased when they'd made port at Crowsmouth. They wanted rum, whores, and gambling—who was Marcas to deny them that?

"Ol' Angus never would'a done this," he overheard more than once. It set his teeth on edge, but he kept quiet. The crew were allowed their displeasure. They'd earned that much in such lean months.

"Are you happy with the way the plan's runnin', Cap'n?" Mr. Dawkins had asked him once a day for the past week.

He wasn't, if he were being honest with himself.

It had seemed simple enough: once they had the king's diplomat they'd go about their business, find a merchant bound for Crakesyde, and send word by way of that ship that Captain Drake wanted to ransom the diplomat back to His Highness. The crew had voted on the kidnapping plot, and it was unanimous to go ahead.

But now?

Now they weren't so happy having to worry about a valuable prisoner. They wanted a real break from sailing, and they wanted the ransom money now instead of later. The latter was impossible at present, but the former easily handled.

"Listen here! I've heard the talk from you lot, and you're all right about us needing a break from cruising. When we make port at Silverwell, we'll take our leave for a few days," Marcas announced to his crew.

"Only that much, Captain?" Morris, the cabin boy, called out from across the deck.

"I'm not wanting you to settle down with any whores, Morris," Marcas shouted back with a smirk.

Some of the crew erupted in laughter at the boy's expense. It was good to see smiles again, and good cheer, no matter how temporary.

∽

EXCITED SHOUTS ERUPTED from above as the ship weighed anchor. Gavin put down his book and peered out the small porthole window in his cell.

Other ships were docked nearby. They'd pulled into port! Finally, he'd have a chance to enact his escape plan. Granted, it wasn't a very good plan, he thought cynically, but it was better than just sitting in a cabin for weeks on end and accepting his fate as a prisoner.

It sounded, from the pounding of feet on deck above, like a mass exodus from the ship. Gavin couldn't help but feel a pang of jealousy. He got up from his hammock and peered through the tiny barred window in the door to his cell. He could see and hear one pirate lamenting her misfortune of having the afternoon watch. Otherwise, the galley was empty, presenting the perfect opportunity for an escape attempt.

"Excuse me! Where are we?" he called out through the little bars.

"Oh, aye, like I'm gonna tells the prisoner what port we's at?" the pirate said and laughed. It was the same old sailor who'd first informed Captain Drake of his arrival back at Crowsmouth.

"So we're at a port then? Not just stopped at some…island somewhere?" Gavin was grasping at straws, he knew, but he had to bank on the pirate guard being as intelligent as she looked.

"Well brush me barnacles, 'e's a bright one, aye?" the pirate said to herself and laughed again, this time doubling over with mirth. "You can belay all them questions, prisoner. Yer lucky I'm even talkin' at you instead of droppin' yer off the side of the ship!"

"I don't think Captain Drake would be very pleased with you if he found you'd got rid of me," Gavin said with a sigh. Already he was tired of this uneven duel of wits. The pirate was so stupid that Gavin would never win at this rate.

"Oh an' why's that? Thinks yer clever does you?" That prompted the pirate to get up from her seat on a small crate and take a few steps towards the door, one hand resting on the hilt of her cutlass.

"Obviously I'm meant to be ransomed to the king or else I'd be dead by now. I'm a dreadfully boring prisoner; the Captain's said as much to me himself." Gavin glared at the pirate through the bars in his door.

"Stow yer gob, prisoner! That's the captain's business an' none of yours!" The guard advanced on the door and glared back through the bars at Gavin.

"What's the matter? Don't you like civil conversation?"

"No, by rights, I don't reckon I do. Now shut yer face before I come in there an' makes you do it meself!"

"But I was enjoying our conversation. You're the first one to really talk to me besides Captain Drake. And, might I add, the king did pay for my place on this ship himself. I've earned the right to be here and chat with whomever I like, by my reasoning." Gavin knew he was pushing it, but he had to. He was left with no choice.

"What fool's gone and broke adrift 'ere? No one's died an' made you captain, you foppish bastard! There's no reasonin' to be done by you, an' I think you knows it!" the guard shouted. Satisfied with her colourful tirade, she turned around and marched back to her previous post, shaking her head as she went.

Gavin bit his lip, trying to think of what to do next. Goading wasn't working very well. Insults probably wouldn't either, not to mention he had no idea what would offend the woman most. Calling her a fool or an idiot would likely make her laugh again.

He stretched out on his hammock and stared up at the low, slatted ceiling. All he could think of then was how very much he'd like to see his sister's smiling face again, to hear her voice. He imagined how excited she'd be to hear the story of his little adventure gone awry, once she was certain he was unharmed. But the truth weighed on him: he'd been kidnapped by pirates and his family had no idea.

It was unusual for Marcas to stay on board the *Ebon Drake* while his crew had all the fun in the taverns. That wasn't to say he was without his rum, but the quiet at the docks in the evening bored him. He looked over at the hourglass he'd overturned just after he'd sent Morris off to find his old friend, Captain Jimmy the Noose. He'd seen Jim's carrack, *The Jaded Jewel*, with its distinct green sails, when they'd pulled into port. Half an hour had passed. Marcas hoped his cabin boy hadn't got himself sidetracked, or he'd have to make an example of him the next morning.

While he waited, he looked over the maps he'd spread out on his table. He'd charted a course that would take them southwest towards Marksport, hopeful they'd be more likely to cross paths with a merchant headed to Crakesyde on the way there. But it would all depend on what sort of information he gathered while he was in Silverwell. It had been three years since he'd had a run-in with the Crimson Queen, and he intended to keep it that way. So much as a hint she'd be in the vicinity or had been recently would be enough cause for Marcas to weigh anchor.

A light rapping at the open doors to his cabin made Marcas look up from his maps and compass.

"Ahoy there, Captain Drake. I hear you've a live one on board and can't get away even to see an old friend!" It was a gruff, familiar voice. Jimmy smiled and walked in at Marcas's nod of recognition.

"Jim! So glad Morris didn't get carried off by some tavern boy before he found you. How've you been? Avoiding the Highbronian gallows, I hope." Marcas stepped out from behind the table and poured his friend a glass of rum.

Jim took a grateful swig and rubbed his scarred, brown neck once he'd swallowed. "Third time's a charm, mate, but four would be pushin' old Lady Luck into an early grave with me. I'd rather die at sea like your old man. Only fitting death for a pirate!"

"Cheers to old Angus Drake! May his name live on longer than ours!" Marcas said with a laugh. He clanked his bottle against Jim's glass before they both took a long drink in toast.

"So, young Mr. Morris says he's sworn to secrecy over what sort of prisoner you're holding in the brig," Jim said with a curious tilt of his head. He plopped down in one of the chairs in the sitting area of the cabin and took another swig of rum. Then his attention was caught by the two portraits propped up against the wall. Only one was fully visible, covering half of the framed canvas behind it, but it was clear that the subject of both paintings was the same: a young redheaded woman in fancy dress, draped in pearls and diamonds.

"My crew wanted to toss those overboard, called them bad luck. So far nothing's happened of course," Marcas said as he gestured at the portraits, catching Jim's line of sight. He shrugged and sat in his favourite chair.

"Marcas. You're telling me you don't know who she is?" Jim gawked at Marcas in amused disbelief.

Marcas shook his head. He had his theories of course, the strongest being that it was Mr. Smith's sister or cousin. The familial resemblance was uncanny.

Jim laughed and slapped his knee, sloshing his rum in the process. "Sink me, mate! I don't know where you got them from, but hang on to them. That there, I'd swear me life on it, is Princess Euphemia of Crakesyde herself!"

Rum spluttered down Marcas's chin, dripping onto his shirt. He swallowed hard and wiped his mouth with the cuff of his sleeve. "You're having me on."

"No, no. I dare swear; that's her!" Jim shook his head and rubbed his throat again.

It felt like a fog had lifted. Fortune had truly smiled down on the *Ebon Drake*. If the girl in the portrait was indeed Princess Euphemia, then that would make her brother Prince Gavin. The crown prince. The *only* prince.

Imaginary piles upon piles of gold coin rushed into Marcas's mind's eye. He could go into early retirement, settle on a little island out in the middle of no-one-knew-where with a smaller vessel meant for leisure. He could get away from it all, pass his beloved ship on to Mr. Dawkins, who he knew would take care of it the way a captain should. Above all else, he could finally, permanently, escape the Crimson Queen and her ilk. It was like a dream unfolding before him; all he had to do was make certain the girl in the painting was the sister of "Mr. Smith." Then he could adjust his plan from there.

"I don't think they'll fetch all that much, mate," Jim said. He eyed Marcas with slight amusement. "Didn't mean to send you chasing mermen there."

"I suppose you're right, but we've hit a hard stretch. Any extra gold will be more than welcomed by my crew."

Jim nodded in complete understanding. "And before you ask, I haven't heard word of Her Royal Lunacy in some time. Lucky for me and my crew, we've avoided her as long as we have. Last port we sailed into up north, heard talk of a ship with red sails being spotted a few weeks before. Said it was headed for Fort Gale. Never stopped at Fort Gale though, so who knows where she could be now, or if that one was even the *Crimson Wake*."

Marcas took another long pull of rum straight from the bottle. No real news was good news, he decided. "Thank you, Jim. Now, tell me, how've things been going for you and the *Jewel*?"

GAVIN WAS startled awake by someone shaking him by the shoulder. He blinked. His eyelids felt like lead weights. Whoever had woken him had lit a candle and set it on the small writing desk at the foot of the hammock.

"Who is it? What's going on?" he asked, his voice coming

out in a sleepy drawl. He covered a yawn with the back of his hand and leaned up to get a better look at the dark shape of a person hovering near him.

"It's Captain Drake. Nothing's going on really, and I'm sorry to wake you like this." The captain sounded genuinely apologetic. He sat down on the trunk situated next to the hammock and rested his arms on his knees.

A quick glance at the door showed Gavin it had been closed again for some semblance of privacy. He wondered what exactly was going on, his head still swimming with strange dreams. The first thought that came to mind was the cabin boy's blatant mentioning of the captain's proclivity to men whenever he brought Gavin meals not taken with the captain. It was something he'd written off as the product of jealousy, as it was clear the boy had an interest in the captain from the way he spoke about him.

"The girl in the portraits, is she your sister?"

The question caught Gavin in the midst of his strange string of thoughts and cut through them easily enough. He was still so very tired, and not being able to fathom any reason to keep the information to himself, he answered truthfully.

"Yes, my younger sister. I wonder... Can I have them back?" Gavin pushed himself up into a sitting position on the hammock, legs crossed, and rested his head in his hand. His eyes began to ease shut, mind drifting off towards another dreamscape.

"That depends, Your Highness."

"On what?" Gavin's eyes shot open at the sound of the other man's voice and then drifted closed again.

"On how much gold the king is willing to spare for the ransom of his son."

"What?" Gavin straightened up so quickly his hammock swayed. Comprehension smacked him in the face. He'd been too comfortable in his role as prisoner. He'd stupidly let down his guard! And for what? Sleep? He glanced at the door again, then at the captain's shadowed face. The man's dark goatee looked sinister in the flickering light of the candle. "I've no idea what you're talking about."

"Don't worry, I won't let on to any of the crew. This is our little secret, *Prince Gavin*." The captain sounded self-satisfied, which only worried Gavin more.

"How…? But the guard? And I'm not even—"

"I dismissed her for the night. And don't even consider trying to escape now. I'm always armed, you know, and I'm not afraid to damage the future king of Crakesyde if he pushes me to it."

Silence filled the little cell of a cabin. Gavin had nothing else to say that might persuade Captain Drake he wasn't who he was. Again, he mentally cursed his father's senility. He'd played the good little prisoner for long enough. He'd been cooperative once he realised he had no real means of escape out on the open water. But he'd had enough.

"My father hates me. I'm convinced he sent me on this ridiculous journey in the hopes I wouldn't come back. So it's likely he won't even pay you any ransom money at all," Gavin said venomously. He slid out of the hammock and crossed his arms over his chest, staring down at the captain. "If you won't let me leave, then get out."

Captain Drake paused for a moment before bursting into a fit of laughter. It wasn't the sort of reaction Gavin expected, and his confidence faltered.

"You think you've earned some sort of authoritative powers over me just because I know who you really are?" Captain Drake asked, flabbergasted. He laughed again. "My ship, my rules. A few weeks and you've forgot what I said on day one! Some king you'll be."

That was it. It was the final straw. Without thinking,

Gavin darted for the door. He barely had the latch lifted before the captain's hand gripped his upper arm painfully tight and pulled him towards the back of the cabin. There was a squeak of metal as the latch slipped back into place.

Captain Drake snatched Gavin to him and held a knife to the side of his neck.

Gavin's eyes went wide as he stared up at the captain's sneering face. One false move could mean his death, no matter how much he might be worth alive. Mere inches separated them, and Gavin could smell alcohol on the pirate's breath. Just another reason for him to hold still and not say anything that might encourage the man to cut him.

Then the captain's lips were on his. Any initial instinct to pull away was shoved down by the cold metal still touching his skin. So he stood there and let Captain Drake kiss him. He tried not to think of how strange it was to be kissed by a man with facial hair. He tried to ignore any comparisons between the pirate and a stable hand he used to steal kisses from. He certainly tried not to kiss back, tried to remember this was not a good thing. No matter how attractive Captain Drake may or may not have been, the man was a pirate keeping him prisoner!

But Gavin failed to notice the knife was gone until the captain's hand ran through his hair, pulling him closer. He nearly panicked, yet the tenderness of the kiss seemed so uncharacteristic, so out of place, that he convinced himself he was dreaming again. The stupid cabin boy had put these thoughts into his head. Now he was dreaming about how the captain must taste of rum, how his hands would feel rough sliding under his shirt and against his own smooth skin. Even the sound of the crew singing shanties off key somewhere outside the little cabin fit into the ridiculous dream.

"Curse it all!" Captain Drake muttered angrily after

pulling away from Gavin. He dashed out of the cabin and locked the door behind him.

Gavin stood there, watching the locked door as if he'd seen a ghost. He touched his fingers to his lips, and as the stamping of boots and chorus of drunken singing and laughter grew louder and louder, Gavin knew he wouldn't be able to fall back to sleep that night.

CHAPTER 4

THE DISTINCT SMELL OF SMOKE WOKE MARCAS FROM AN already fitful sleep. At first, he wasn't sure if he was imagining the smell, but then Morris burst through the doors to his cabin in a panic.

"Cap'n! Cap'n! There's a fire on deck! Fire!" Morris squawked, his voice cracking as he shouted.

"Damn it, boy! Get out there and help put it out!" Marcas commanded. He jumped to his feet and didn't bother to put on his shirt or coat.

He chased after the cabin boy and saw a coil of rope near the mizzenmast was ablaze. The remnants of a shattered lantern were strewn off to the side of it. *Kerosene.* Some idiot had dropped the lantern. Or maybe the wind? Whatever had happened, Marcas decided while shouting orders to all hands on deck, he would find the culprit if there was one and give them twenty lashings. There was no question about his mood this night.

"The wind's makin' it spread!" Morris shouted, still panicked and not doing much to help save the ship or his fellow crew members.

"Stow your gab and help Canker and Bones with the bloody buckets!" Marcas shouted, gesturing angrily. He shoved the boy towards the line of pirates pulling water up from the waves before joining them himself. He wouldn't lose his ship because of some adolescent who wasn't worth a damn in a crisis. And he wouldn't lose his ship to some damn fire!

A calm in the wind allowed the men to douse the final embers. The coil of rope and much of the deck were soaked, but the fire was no more. A cheer sounded on board as Mr. Dawkins shouted back down the line.

"She's saved! Good work, mates!"

"Excellent work!" Marcas shouted. But any relief he felt was hidden by the rage still evident in his voice. "Now! Who's responsible for this mess?"

The crew looked around at one another. Some busied themselves with checking the damage done to the ropes while others set about cleaning the mess itself. No one spoke.

"Did no one, not a one of you, see what started the fire?" Marcas snarled. Someone had caused the fire, accidentally no doubt, but that recklessness would not be tolerated. He had his suspicions, but he wanted a confession. He was not in the habit of punishing the wrong crew member.

"Most've us were below decks, takin' our turns to sleep, Cap'n," Bones said. He shrugged apologetically at his captain.

"Most," Marcas parroted his bosun. He looked around at his crew again, attempting to look each one of them in the eyes as he spoke. "I know whose watch it was, so don't count your captain a fool! If it was an accident of the wind, just speak the truth and be done with it. I can't fault nature for her whims any more than I can the sea!"

Some of them laughed, but a good majority didn't. An awkward silence settled on board until, finally, Morris walked up to his captain with his head bowed.

"I uh… 'Twas me, sir. I tripped an' dropped my lantern. I din't mean—"

Marcas grabbed him by the throat and lifted him up off the deck, cutting short whatever apologies he'd been trying to make.

"The next time I ask whose fault it is," Marcas growled through his teeth, "I expect the culprit to answer me straight away. I have no time for blundering fools who bite their tongues!"

Morris whimpered and made a strange coughing sound. Captain Drake dropped him and let him splutter for all of two seconds before pointing at the bosun and the quartermaster.

"Bones! Mr. Dawkins! Give young Mr. Morris here twenty lashes!"

The boy cried out and then shoved his fist against his mouth. He knew he'd earn more lashes if he made so much as another sound.

Marcas wasn't interested in watching the proceedings. He knew the boy would be days recovering, but it would be well worth keeping him below decks and out of everyone else's way. The boy was a hazard, not only to himself, but to everyone on board. If he kept it up, he'd be dropped off at the next port with his cut of the gold they had, which was nothing to crow about.

Marcas slammed his cabin door shut as the first crack of the bosun's whip slapped against Morris's back.

∽

ANOTHER THREE DAYS PASSED UNEVENTFULLY. Morris was more careful than ever to lie low, keep quiet, and stay out of Marcas's way.

Marcas peered out over Siren's Deep, scanning the

horizon through his spyglass. Nothing but the sea ahead of them. It was disheartening. They hadn't come across a single other ship in nearly a fortnight and weren't due to reach the next port until three more days had passed. That was *if* the wind held out for them.

He felt alone among his own crew. Very alone. All thanks to the secret he kept, his ticket to a much better place in the history books. Because no other pirate had done something so amazing as kidnapping a prince. Not just any prince, but the crown prince of Crakesyde! Even his father, Deadeye Angus Drake, had never pulled off anything so fantastic. Angus had been much more focused on treasure, on making sure his crew were contented with their unpredictable lives. If Marcas was honest with himself, he'd have to grudgingly admit Deadeye Drake had been a much better captain than his son. That was an admittance he'd kept shoved down for years, however, and if he had his wont, that very idea would be washed away by the brilliance of his ransoming back the prince.

"Would ya lookit that!" one of the crew exclaim behind him. It sounded like Canker's craggy old voice. Marcas abandoned his spyglass and turned around to see what was so remarkable.

The pirates on deck were all looking up at the top of the main mast, pointing. A huge white bird settled in for a landing on the crow's nest.

"Brilliant," Marcas muttered under his breath as he eyed the massive albatross. Just what he needed! Something else for the crew to hang on to with every superstitious bone in their bodies. He'd never had an albatross anywhere near his ship before, and he couldn't help feeling agitated that this one decided, out of nowhere, to use the mast as a resting spot.

"What should we do?" one of the crew said.

"Jest leave it be, I reckons; leave it be," another replied.

"We oughtta makes it leave before somethin' happens to it!" Canker said. Without another word she started the climb up to the crow's nest.

"Leave it!" one of the others shouted. "You'll make it angry!"

"Oi, yeah, an' the spirits of the beyond'll curse you fer touchin' it!" another called up after the old pirate.

Marcas had tried to ignore the little scene, but it was distracting the crew from more serious things. Like gathering their prisoner for lunch with their captain. He hadn't bothered "inviting" the prince to meals with him since that night at Silverwell. The incident in the cell had played a little more heavily on his thoughts than he'd meant it to. He was a man. He had urges, and unlike the rest of his crew, he hadn't allowed himself to leave his ship while they'd been docked at Silverwell. Then he'd let said urges get the best of him. For just a moment.

Canker's ascent to the crow's nest caught his attention again. She'd nearly reached her goal. Marcas wasn't sure what it was she intended to do to persuade the bird to leave, but figured it might be entertaining to watch after all. Once it was over, he'd have Mr. Dawkins fetch the prisoner.

The prisoner who he couldn't deny was attractive. Gavin wasn't tanned from years in the sun and salt air, and his hazel eyes were very expressive. The red hair, he thought, was an asset, not a curse. But Marcas had his own code he lived by, instilled in him by his father. He might be a pirate, but that didn't mean he was just some cruel beast. He was a man, and he treated those he respected with the sort of regard he wished returned to him. Marcas wanted to be known in the history books as the most infamous pirate ever, not the most bloodthirsty or cutthroat. He'd made a misstep, gone too far, and he'd have to hope his prisoner would forgive his mistake.

He would woo the prince, he decided. His charms had never failed him before, so there was no reason for him to doubt his ultimate success. Perhaps it was fortuitous they hadn't yet come across a merchant ship, even if it meant a slightly restless crew. They had plans to make berth at Marksport before the week was out as it stood. They could pick up better leads from there, and the crew could relax again.

Up in the crow's nest, arms waved while shooing sounds and squawking filled the air. Great white wings flapped wildly; then Canker cried out and arched back, away from the bird.

As if it happened in slow motion, the old pirate fell towards the deck. The crew scattered, scrambling to find something, anything, to break her fall. Marcas dashed towards them to help but was too late.

Canker smacked into the deck, her neck twisted at a strange angle.

"It's bad luck! All's bad luck! We've done something to make the old gods curse us!" Mr. Dawkins said, voice shaking. He took his hat off his head and held it to his chest as he looked down at his fallen crewmate.

"Next time one of you has it in their head to go on some fool's errand in the name of superstition, you'll get twenty lashings from me personally," Marcas announced, his voice flat. "Bones, Mr. Dawkins, please prepare our friend here for her final rest."

He felt the warmth drain out of his face. He needed something to take his mind somewhere else. He needed a drink.

"You there." Marcas spotted Morris in the little crowd now on deck. Some of the crew had come up from below to see what the commotion was about. The boy looked aghast and shook his head, backing up as the captain approached him.

"Twasn't me, Captain! Honest I is!"

Marcas sighed and grabbed him by the shoulder before he could run off like a scared mouse. The boy flinched but stayed put. "I know, Morris. I've got eyes. Now, I want you to fetch Mr. Smith to my cabin for me. Tell Cook to send us up some lunch, and then help Mr. Dawkins with whatever he asks. Understood?"

"Yes, sir," Morris said and nodded once.

"There's a good lad," Marcas said, offering him a strained smile. The cabin boy dashed off to do as he was told.

CHAPTER 5

"Why was there blood on deck? What's going on?" Gavin asked once he was alone with Captain Drake in his quarters. It had been days since he'd seen him at all, and he looked haggard. The loud noises he'd heard from his cell weren't positive sounding, and the blood he'd seen some of the crew mopping up on deck had sent a chill through him.

"Sit, please," Captain Drake said. His voice was tight, forced, and every movement he made looked precisely measured, unlike his usually languid gestures.

Gavin thought to protest the order, but he was afraid the captain's fuse might be dangerously short. So he sat down in the chair that didn't sink in the middle.

The captain poured a single glass of rum and then drank at length from the bottle. He handed the glass to Gavin a moment later. After another swig from his bottle, he sat down in his favourite chair, the one beside Gavin's.

"Do you believe the old gods are real?" Captain Drake asked as he frowned at his bottle. He tilted it in a circular motion, swirling the dark rum.

"I've certainly never seen any evidence of gods," Gavin

said, his frown matching Drake's. They were the stuff of fairy stories. Tales told to teach children early lessons about the value of human life and safety in the wider world. "I know some folk still believe the gods used to exist, but I'm not among them."

"Do you believe in superstitions?" the captain asked, glancing over at Gavin.

Gavin blinked, not understanding where the captain's questions had come from, and ran his thumbs over the rim of his glass. "I don't suppose so, no. Does this have to do with my having red hair?"

Captain Drake shook his head and looked at the far wall of the cabin. "I know you're my prisoner, and there's no reason for me to be candid with you at any turn. But if I don't speak freely with some sane person about the state of my crew, I may go mad myself."

Gavin's brows furrowed. Had things really got that bad? He seemed to miss much more than fresh air down in his little cell. This had to be some trick of the captain's. Some new angle to show Gavin that he could be trusted. A pirate? Trustworthy? The mere idea was laughable. But if the captain wanted to play a game, Gavin would have to participate. He'd failed to make his way off the *Ebon Drake* while they'd been docked—and even then, he'd realised he'd have nowhere to run. Nowhere to hide for long. He hadn't known which port town they'd arrived at and assumed it was one of the islands of the Deep. It had likely been a pirate-run township, one where he'd have found no one willing to go against Captain Drake unless he revealed his identity and opened himself to a new captor. His only option was to play along, so he nodded in understanding.

"My crew...most of them, you've no doubt seen, are old. Men and women who've been at sea longer than either one of us have been alive. Sailors who've seen their fair share of strange things, dark events, death. So it's no surprise they've come to be more and more superstitious over time. More leery of any ill omens, those real and imagined." The captain took another long pull from his bottle of rum. He exhaled a heavy breath and turned his gaze to Gavin again.

And Gavin felt as if those green eyes could see through to the very core of his being. He sank back into his chair and took a tentative sip of the rum he'd been poured. It was very different from the wines he was used to sipping at home, but swallowed the coarse liquor despite his palate's protest. He cleared his throat and wondered if the captain was going to continue or if he was waiting for some sort of response.

"Are they being unreasonable? Irrational?" Gavin asked, choosing his words carefully. He didn't want to take a chance of saying something offensive.

"Irrational, yes. It's worrisome and it cost me one of my best sailors today," Captain Drake said, sounding entirely sober.

The conversation was interrupted by a knock on the door. Captain Drake told the person to enter, and Gavin was pleased to see it was the cabin boy, followed by two other crew members, bringing lunch to the table. He watched them from his seat, but didn't dare get up. His eyes strayed to the open door. Captain Drake reached over and put a hand on his shoulder. He could feel his skin turn to gooseflesh at the subtle warning.

"Looks like Cook's outdone himself on your behalf, Mr. Smith," the captain said with a nod and a smile at the crew as they ducked back out of the cabin. Once the door was closed again, he got up and locked it, as was usual of their meetings; then he put the key back into an inside pocket of his vest. "Eat your fill, Gavin. I know you've been living off slop and hard tack for days."

At the captain's orders, Gavin thought bitterly. The food

he'd been given was filling but had minimal taste. It left him looking forward to meals with the captain, but he guessed that was the point of the entire arrangement. He moved to join the captain at the table and tried to ignore the use of his real name. He much preferred to be Mr. Smith. But as Gavin stared down at his empty plate and the food laid out on the table, he recalled the captain's words just before the food had been brought in. It dulled his appetite.

"Someone's died today," Gavin said and, though he'd intended it to be a question, it came out as a concerned statement. He'd seen the blood on the deck. The fleeting hope of some bloody but non-fatal brawl between crew members had been quashed.

"Yes," the captain replied. He slowly put food on his own plate and took another swig of rum. "The crew and their fear of some blasted bird! It's madness. A waste!"

Gavin nodded, not understanding what a fear of birds had to do with a sailor dying that day. But he didn't feel he was owed a full explanation of a tender subject. He was just a prisoner. He doubted he should spare any sentiment or kind emotions for pirates anyway. But pirates were people too; they were human just the same as he was. They had feelings, no matter how much they might pretend not to. Gavin wasn't sure how to feel, so he put some food on his plate and started to eat.

"I need you to pen a letter," Captain Drake said after an extended silence. "A letter to your father explaining you've been kidnapped and that a hefty ransom is expected in exchange for your safe return."

Gavin looked up from his plate and watched the captain. The man studied him in return, but already his eyes seemed red-tinged from too much drink, or perhaps stress or emotion over his loss. There was no way to tell.

"What if he sends nothing?" Gavin had to ask. He set his

fork back on his plate, tines down. The command brought up all manner of doubts. The ones he'd been having fitful sleep over. The ones where the captain grew tired of him and the king's lack of response and finally dropped him overboard to satisfy his crew.

"Don't be ridiculous. You're the crown prince of the largest kingdom in the bloody world! He'd be a madman not to offer something," Captain Drake said. There was a hint of laughter to his voice, but all traces of a smile were short-lived.

Gavin looked Captain Drake in the eyes, to make sure his captor could see he wasn't lying. "My father is old and very senile. I've been of the mind that he's lost his over the past five years. I simply wish to know if you plan to kill me in the event he ignores my letter or offers a pittance for my return."

Captain Drake frowned then. For a moment, Gavin thought he might've actually got through the pirate's thick skull. But when the man stood up from the table and swaggered around it, he had a feeling his words hadn't made so much as a dent. The captain leaned on the table next to Gavin and smirked down at him.

"You, my friend, are a fantastic liar."

"I was speaking the truth. I'm sorry my father's declining mental health is amusing to you." Gavin found his regal demeanor had returned in full, and he wasn't sorry for it.

"Your problem is you don't know how to relax, Gavin." Captain Drake pointed to the glass of rum he'd poured earlier. It was still more than half-full. "You can start by not being afraid of alcohol."

Gavin bristled as heat crept up his face. He wasn't stupid, and Captain Drake knew that. He wasn't about to drown his sorrows and forget who he was, what was going on, and what the consequences of doing every stupid thing that came into his head would be. He'd been drunk before, and it hadn't been pretty. He'd made several obvious passes at one of his sister's suitors—a member of the current King's Council, at that. Luckily Effie had thought the man a bore and found the entire situation hilarious. His father, on the other hand, had been annoyed at his lack of propriety. Whatever large amounts of hard liquor did for other people, it turned him into a lecher. Not a fact that brought him pride.

"I doubt that will make my problems disappear," Gavin said as lightly as he could manage. But he couldn't keep his sarcasm at bay. "I dare say it would make more of them."

"Dare you? And why's that?" Captain Drake asked. His shift back to his normal arrogant self seemed complete. He grinned broadly and raised an eyebrow at Gavin's comment. "Afraid you'll do something you'll regret?"

"Yes. Like another poor attempt at an escape," Gavin said quickly. His cheeks burned as his mind raced to what had happened the last time he'd tried such a thing. He decided he'd definitely had too much to drink already and should hold his tongue for the rest of this ridiculous visit.

"I rather enjoyed that. And if I'm not mistaken, so did you," Captain Drake said. Rum obviously made him lecherous as well.

Gavin pressed his lips together. He ignored all of the excellent and not so excellent retorts that flooded his mind. He wouldn't let this situation get away from him! The captain had told Gavin what he wanted him to do. He'd go back to his cabin, write the letter as requested, and that would be the end of it. He most certainly wouldn't turn into some wanton sex slave who only existed for Captain Drake's carnal amusement.

The captain, however, was unfazed by Gavin's sudden silence. "It's all right, you know," he said. "I'm very handsome. Or so I've been told."

Gavin rolled his eyes and went back to staring at the food

on his plate. He had to think of some way to end the luncheon prematurely. Some way that didn't involve him getting drunk or doing anything lascivious. All he had to work with was a fork.

"You can't give me the silent treatment forever, Gavin," Captain Drake said with a light laugh. He sauntered over to his favourite chair again and sat down unceremoniously, one leg draped over an arm of the chair. He beckoned with both hands. "Why don't you come here? Let's chat about your stubborn insistence about your father being a complete loony. If he's *really* that far off, I'll bet I could help you deal with him."

Gavin continued to ignore the pirate, no matter how much the man's words incensed him. He closed his eyes and turned his head far enough to put the captain out of his peripheral vision. He was certain he was in no physical danger while in Captain Drake's presence, yet his mental and emotional health were other beasts entirely.

"Look, I didn't mean to upset you," Captain Drake backtracked. He sounded somewhat sincere. "I shared important introspective details of my life with you…and I suppose I felt you might do the same. The dark inner workings of His Royal Highness, now there's something no man gets to bear witness to…ever."

"There's nothing dark about my inner workings," Gavin said after another awkward silence. It was the truth. He was a terribly boring human being. He liked books and fine art, the theatre, and fencing. He abhorred social dramatics, like the sort he was being forced through now, and he was never going to be able to prove he'd be a decent king if his life kept on in the same direction for much longer. He turned in his chair and faced the captain. "Can I please return to my cabin now?"

Captain Drake shrugged. "If you agree to write the

ransom letter without further whinging about how much daddy doesn't love you."

"You arse!" Gavin shouted. He leapt up and marched over to the captain angrily. He reached for the hilt of Captain Drake's cutlass, intent on drawing it before the pirate could register what was going on in his alcohol-addled mind.

Captain Drake moved quickly, blocking Gavin's hand and gripping it tightly. In one fluid motion, he rose to his feet and twisted the arm around to Gavin's back. He marched Gavin up to the nearest wall, shoved his face against the wood, and pushed his arm up painfully.

Gavin had been played the fool.

The injured whimper that escaped Gavin's throat only served to make him embarrassed on top of bested. He bit his lip to keep any further pathetic utterances at bay.

"Looks like you don't need much rum to make you do stupid things after all," Captain Drake said right into Gavin's ear.

The prince shuddered as a chill from Drake's breath raced down his spine. He hoped whatever horrible torture about to be inflicted upon him would be over soon.

"I know you're tired of my brand of hospitality. I know you'd fling yourself overboard at the mere suggestion of a possible escape. But there's one thing you and your short fuse keep forgetting: we're in the middle of Siren's Deep. There's nowhere for you to go in the sea but down. Even the strongest of men's arms would give out before he so much as sighted land," Drake said in a voice too calm for comfort.

"You only want me alive so you can have your gold and your way with me," Gavin struggled to say. He swallowed hard and tried to tilt his head to the side, arch his back ever so slightly, move just enough to ease the pressure on his arm. But it didn't help. The movement encouraged Drake to pin him more firmly to the wall. He grimaced with a pained grunt.

"And you think all pirates are alike. Stupid drunkards with a lust for treasure, fucking, and little else," the captain said, his voice betraying a sneer. "While I'm happy to know my reputation precedes me, you'd be sorely mistaken to think so many stories are all there is to Marcas Drake. I suggest you stop underestimating me and start enjoying your little cruise while it lasts."

Was he mad? Gavin mentally scoffed at the idea of his captivity being a pleasure cruise of some sort. He wasn't in the habit of being kidnapped by pirates, so he had no other experiences to compare this one to. Yet based on all accounts he'd heard of people being locked away on pirate ships, the captain was right. He'd been treated relatively well. He wasn't starving. He hadn't been beaten. The only thing he really had to worry about was whether or not the captain was going to force him into another sexually charged interlude.

Forced, yes; it was only because he'd been held at knifepoint, he told himself yet again. Eyes shut tight, he knew he had to stop thinking any kind thoughts about his captor. Perhaps Gavin was the one who'd gone mad? That's what happened to people who were kept in small spaces too long, wasn't it?

Slowly, the pressure on Gavin's arm was released. As the tension in his shoulder and elbow relaxed to a comfortable level, he wondered if the captain would object to him dropping his arm to his side. There was no way to know without asking or trying, but he enjoyed the strange silence. He wished Captain Drake would step away and let him go back to his seat. But the other man's breath was still warm on his ear and neck.

Just as Gavin was about to break the silence, which had

grown too awkward too quickly, one of Captain Drake's hands came away from the wall and caressed his cheek. The same hand ran down his shoulder and arm, pulling the trapped limb from its prison between their bodies.

Gavin froze, as he had in his own cabin. Drake's arm wrapped around his middle in an odd half hug. This was it, the moment he'd been dreading. The captain would have his way with him and then toss him back to his cell until he desired him again. His luck being what it was, Gavin wouldn't even have a chance to steal the captain's key before it was all over.

"I enjoy your company, Gavin," Captain Drake said. "I don't enjoy your foolish attempts to escape or kill me. So tell me what I need to do to win your trust, to prove to you that I'm interested in you, not just how much gold you're worth."

Gavin's eyes shot open. The captain was indeed mad! Stark raving mad! How could he reply to such a request? It had to be a trick. Another chance for the captain to turn his words and the situation around on him so he could have a good laugh.

"Why should I believe your sincerity?" Gavin asked, eyeing Captain Drake warily out of the corner of his eye. He paused before speaking again, giving the captain a chance to reply.

The rum must have finally caught up with Drake, because he took a moment to think. As Gavin seized the chance to speak again, he forced his voice to remain calm and collected. He was too afraid of what the captain might do if he angered him too much, but he wanted to push a bit, just enough to ruin his enjoyment of Gavin's company.

"You've kept me as your pet prisoner for weeks, kissed me at knifepoint, practically broken my arm, and at present you have me stuck forcibly to a wall while you're, no doubt, biding your time before doing…unspeakable things to me." A stifled laugh from the captain didn't stop Gavin. "You've certainly given me no reason to trust you. You've lied to me from the moment I met you. And if you were really interested in me as a person, then you'd treat me as a guest on your ship. If you were interested in befriending me—and I find that notion laughable—you would at the very least be honest with me."

Gavin could just make out what looked like a smile on Captain Drake's face.

"If I give you my word that from this moment forward you'll be treated as a guest on my ship, I want your word in return. I want you to swear you won't interfere with my crew. That you won't harm anyone on board or the *Ebon Drake* itself. And swear that you won't dive overboard and hope a mermaid has pity on you."

Gavin took as deep a breath as was possible given the situation. The idea this entire thing was somehow a setup rang out in his mind. But he was interested in seeing the way the ship worked on a daily basis. He wanted to look over the open sea and feel completely surrounded by it. No more peering furtively out of a tiny porthole window, and he thought if he was free to roam the ship he might just be able to pretend he *was* on a pleasure cruise.

"You have my word, Captain," Gavin said.

Captain Drake released him.

The pirate grabbed his bottle of rum off the table and took a seat in his chair again. He raised an eyebrow at Gavin, who still stood near the wall uncertainly, rubbing his shoulder.

"Would you like to attend the funeral at dusk? I can let my crew know about the change in arrangements then."

This time Gavin was taken aback. The earlier events of the afternoon hadn't escaped the captain after all. Gavin was glad. It meant the man was human, that he had a heart in there under the lies, likely swimming in a sea of rum. While his immediate reaction was that, no, he didn't want to pay his respects to someone who'd helped kidnap him, he had to give the offer thought. It was an easy decision in the end. He had a heart himself, and why would he want to ruin any chances he had of allowing the captain and crew to feel amiable towards him?

"Yes, of course," Gavin said.

"Oh yeah, miss, the *Ebon Drake* was 'round here 'bout a fortnight ago. If I'm rememberin' right o' course," the wench said with a grin. She looked at the five gold pieces in her hand again in disbelief. "Hard ship to miss with its bein' black an' all. I heard one o' the crew say they was headed back towards Highbron again. Goin' round an' round. Said he was right sick of it, an' I can't says I blame him."

"You're so right! And such a delightful girl too," the Crimson Queen said with a light laugh. She pulled the girl into a sideways embrace with one arm and walked her over to her first mate. He leaned against the bar of Silverwell's famous Lucky Coin Inn. "Now, Arreid's the one I was telling you about."

"Ooh!" The wench's eyes lit up. She bit her lip, trying to play coy, and looked Arreid up and down. "You're right, miss, he really is handsome! Twenty times more handsome than any o' them old codgers what came off the *Ebon Drake!*"

Looking at the Crimson Queen, Arreid rolled his eyes and gave her a tired look. He pretended to not be interested in other women for her sake, she knew. At least when she wasn't playing with them. But variety was the spice of life, and she couldn't have him getting bored of her or wondering what he might be missing elsewhere.

"Oh come off it, Arreid! Don't be such a spoilsport! She just told me everything I wanted to know about that amazing ship I've been trying to see for so long. We're so close now, and all thanks to our little friend." The Crimson Queen whispered in the girl's ear while keeping her eye on Arreid. Giving the girl a few tips on what the man enjoyed best would be his gift for suggesting they check Silverwell for the elusive Captain Drake.

The Crimson Queen's smile renewed as she watched the wench lead Arreid away to somewhere more private. She finished the rum in her mug and slammed it down on the bar upside down. Now it was her turn to find a little paid company of her own. She held out hope her good fortune would be complete, and whichever one she found to her liking had also been to Captain Drake's liking.

With him evading her for so long, there was no such thing as too much information.

CHAPTER 6

Marcas had always liked the simplicity of a burial at sea. No digging, no coffin to build, no concern for marking the final resting place of the deceased. The sea would take the body and give it to her denizens as nourishment. But that didn't mean he liked burying any of his crew. Especially a crew member who'd been loyal, not only to his father's name, but to Marcas himself. He mentally cursed Canker's stupidity even while he was grateful for the woman's hard work.

A few words, a long moment of silence, and then the crew pulled back the flaps of extra sailcloth covering the body and hoisted her up over the railing. A slight tilt of the sailcloth sent the body over the side and into the water with a splash. The chain shot attached to the body's ankles did its job and Canker sank out of sight beneath the passing waves.

Before the crew could get back to their business, Marcas commanded their attention.

"Comrades all, stand by!" He watched until all eyes were on him, including Gavin's. "I heard some grumblings before we paid our respects, all of them about Mr. Smith's presence here, and felt I ought to explain the reasons for it. It's no secret we've had difficulty finding a proper ship to carry Mr. Smith's ransom letter back to Crakesyde, and as it stands, he might be with us much longer than any of us could have anticipated. Since he's been such an excellent sport during his duration as our prisoner, without so much as an escape attempt, I've struck a deal with him. Mr. Smith is not to injure any crew on this ship, nor the ship herself. And he's also sworn not to fling himself overboard or try slitting his own throat just to spite us. From this day forward, Mr. Smith shall be our honoured guest, seeing as he's one of the king's men and acted as such a gentleman thus far."

There were plenty of shocked and slack-jawed faces among the crew. Marcas had expected as much but kept on as if nothing at all was amiss. Once he'd set his mind to something, no matter how ridiculous it might seem later, he felt compelled to carry out whatever it was until completion. This deal was all part of a greater scheme to be completed before the prince's ransom arrived.

"But 'e'll get in our way, Captain," one of the men commented.

"An' wot if 'e starts gettin' the idea 'e's one of us?"

"Or what if he's a spy and he goes and tells the king all the places we've been?"

Marcas raised an eyebrow and looked over at Gavin. The look he gave him was open appraisal, and not in the fashion he typically looked him over. He looked back at his men, his expression serious.

"Who here thinks Mr. Smith is a royal spy?" Marcas asked. Two hands shot up. Then three more. "Where's your proof?"

None of the accusers spoke. They looked back and forth amongst one another and ultimately came up with a lot of shrugging.

"We can just forget everything if—" Gavin began.

"No! I made a promise, as did you, and I intend to uphold my end of the bargain. I only hope, for your sake, you intend to keep yours," Marcas said firmly. He wasn't backing down, and not just because he didn't want his crew to think their guest had any sway over him, though he certainly wanted to maintain that he was in control of the situation. "There's no proof against your character, Mr. Smith, and until such a time as there is, which there won't be, please enjoy the comforts of the *Ebon Drake*."

Gavin's face was priceless. He looked as though he'd changed his mind after seeing the crew's reaction to his no longer being a mere prisoner. But it was too late.

Now all they needed to do was find a damn merchant ship to strike a bit of terror into, one that'd race straight to Crakesyde without reservations or counter-schemes, and everything would be perfect again.

GAVIN COULDN'T GET ENOUGH of the sight of endless water in all directions, the sea spray, or the sound of the sails as the wind kicked up. Now he could walk around the upper decks of the ship and observe how the crew did their jobs. He could breathe the salty air, which was much more pleasant than the stuffy smells that accumulated below decks. He could even chat with the captain, who maintained a civil manner, and share all of his meals with him.

It had only been two days since he'd cut the strange deal with Captain Drake, and with the ransom letter written and out of the way, it seemed easier for the pirate to see Gavin as his guest.

"I still can't believe you brought half a trunk full of books on a sea voyage," Captain Drake said as they finished their evening meal.

"I like to read. There's also the fact that I had no idea how long I was expected to stay in Highbron and wanted to ensure I'd have my favourite books." Gavin sipped at his rum. There was still caution on his part regarding the liquor, but there seemed to be a lot more of it available on board than fresh water. "I wish I'd brought more, seeing as I've already read them all."

"I'm impressed," Captain Drake said. "I guess I've never been terribly interested in reading for pleasure."

"I wouldn't think you'd have much time for it," Gavin said. He would keep any curiosity about how literate the pirate was to himself.

"You'd be right," Captain Drake agreed.

"Well, thank you again for your company. You're awfully agreeable for an infamous pirate," Gavin said with a grin. He stood and prepared to head back to his cabin for the night.

That agreeable nature made it difficult for Gavin to picture the man doing many of the dastardly things that had been written about him. He had particular trouble envisioning Captain Drake killing anyone, even though he knew he must have at some point. Marcas Drake had to be the strangest pirate in the entire world. Gavin had to wonder if it was because of his age, or maybe he was just less interested than other pirates in committing horrendous crimes.

Although there was no doubting the man's adeptness at manipulation, and Gavin had to spare a stray thought for concern over Drake's agreeableness being a performance for Gavin's sole benefit. But whatever it was, he appreciated the change and felt it kindest to take the man's good will at face value. They'd struck a deal, and the captain was honouring it with aplomb.

"I hope you'll keep those sorts of thoughts to yourself once you're back home, telling tales of your fantastic voyage," Captain Drake said. His expression was dark, but he laughed.

"I'll make up some terrible deeds to keep your name properly sullied." Gavin laughed too. "Good night, Captain."

"Sleep well," Captain Drake said. He got up from his seat and grabbed the bottle of rum off the table. There was something about his demeanour that had changed.

Gavin hoped he hadn't made the captain angry by calling him nice, in so many words. It would be nothing for him to claim Gavin tried to kill him and set him back to being a prisoner again. Gavin enjoyed the freedoms allowed him with their new arrangement, and while the crew didn't seem at all happy about him wandering freely around the ship, they had taken to ignoring him. Even Morris wouldn't speak to him anymore.

After leaving the captain's cabin, Gavin wondered at the fact that Captain Drake hadn't made any more attempts to seduce him. Of course, he hadn't made any more attempts to escape either, but he hardly thought there was a genuine correlation between the two. Other than an excuse for close physical proximity.

The evening air was cool, and Gavin was glad he had on one of the ridiculous outfits his sister had picked out for him. It had a long-sleeved shirt under a long coat, which countered the chill cutting through his knee breeches and hose. He hated modern fashion, but the plain clothes he'd worn earlier in the voyage had become his sleeping clothes.

It wasn't much warmer below deck, though the blanket on his hammock would help. But he didn't get any farther than the bottom of the stairs.

"Mr. Smith, a word?"

Mr. Dawkins caught Gavin by surprise in the near darkness, but after recovering from being startled, he nodded. "Yes, of course."

"See, I've got this problem an' I been thinkin' you could help me with it," the quartermaster said. He motioned for

Gavin to follow him a few steps, as if there was some sort of privacy to be had farther away from the stairs.

"Oh? Well I'll be glad to help in any way I can. I know I haven't been of any practical—"

An object smacked into the back of Gavin's head, and he fell into complete darkness.

"This is mutiny!" Marcas shouted at the top of his lungs. He struggled with every ounce of strength he could muster, but Bones had tied his wrists together behind his back too tightly, and the larger pirate was strong as an ox. He'd been caught off guard and felt like a complete idiot because of it. His pistols were strapped to his chest as usual, and his cutlass was at his side. Still, it had been far too easy for his own crew members, three of them no less, to wrest his arms behind his back and bind him. *Far* too easy.

The big, bald pirate pulled Marcas by the arm, tugging him out of his own cabin and onto the main deck. Most of the crew had assembled, and many of them were carrying lanterns to brighten up the darkness. There were heavy clouds in the sky obscuring the sliver of moon. Jeers and cheers could be heard throughout the small crowd.

"I found 'em! I found 'em! Mr. Dawkins, he was right o' course!" Morris shouted excitedly, his voice cracking as he ran out of the captain's cabin. He held the two portraits of Princess Euphemia high so the other men could see.

"Cut 'em to shreds! Then throw 'em overboard!" Mr. Dawkins called out from somewhere at the back of the crowd. The men made way for him, and he gave Marcas a disgusted look when he was close enough. "It should've been done when we left Crowsmouth!"

"You're mutineers, all of you! And over some bloody

paintings? You're all completely fucking mad!" Marcas snarled. He tried to break free of Bones's grasp again, but the larger pirate held his arm tighter.

"It's over all this bad luck, Marcas," Mr. Dawkins said, making sure to draw out the first name of his former captain. "We've had enough of your lackadaisical attitude towards piratin' these last three years. We're sick of runnin' scared from the Crimson Queen like a mess of cowards. You've cost us enough plunder by turnin' tail every time you hear that witch's name!"

"I've done all that to save us, you realise," Marcas growled, spittle flying from his lips. "She's psychotic!"

"And she's after you! Not us, not the *Ebon Drake*, just *you*, Marcas." Mr. Dawkins laughed and drew his cutlass. He aimed the blade at Marcas's face and shrugged one shoulder, as if he were sorry he was commandeering the man's ship and crew, his livelihood, his life. "You used to be a great captain, Marcas. We would've followed ye to the ends of the world and beyond, but somehows the queen's addled your brains. Now this kidnappin' plot that's goin' absolutely nowhere!"

"If you'll all just wait until we find a ship bound for Crakesyde—"

"No! That's the whole point, Marcas! Your scheme's brought us nothing but bad luck! A redhead on board our ship, and all with a captain who's blind to the misfortune the wretch brought with him! We haven't even seen another vessel at sea since we left Crowsmouth! Then the fire, and our old friend who's now lost to the Deep. How can you not see it, Marcas? How can you pretend all's well?"

"He's buggering the prisoner's how!" one of the crew shouted.

"Aye, Marcas, we know you well enough," Mr. Dawkins said with a fresh smirk.

"I have not," Marcas called out, loud enough for everyone present to hear. His patience ran thin. This was completely ridiculous! He hadn't been such a bad captain. Sure he'd been looking out for his own best interests, but that's what a pirate was *supposed* to do. He couldn't be held at fault for their dry spell.

"Well then you've been covetin' the idea. Same difference when yer mixin' business with pleasure. You unnerstand." Mr. Dawkins dropped his cutlass from its threatening position near Marcas's neck. "Bones, toss him in the boat with his little mate. Maybe Marcas is right! Maybe they'll spot a merchant ship afore we do an' he can keep all the ransom money to hisself!"

The crew roared with laughter, and all further protests from Marcas were drowned out by the din. Bones did as he was told and dropped Marcas unceremoniously into one of the lifeboats. As the boat lowered, Marcas saw Gavin laid out at the other end of the small craft, unconscious. There was a lit lantern, a bottle of rum, a bit of rope, and some hard tack biscuits beside the redhead.

"Don't worry, Cap'n!" Morris shouted down. He leaned so far over the railing it looked like he might fall overboard. "There's an island just to the northwest! We left the oars in the boat!"

More peals of laughter sounded from the deck of the ship, which might as well have been miles away. Soon enough the *Ebon Drake* sailed off to what Marcas could only guess was the southeast. His compass rested in his jacket pocket, so he'd know as soon as he could get his hands free. Thankfully, they hadn't taken any of his personal effects before tying him up and setting him adrift.

He kicked Gavin's shoe a few times.

"Oi, wake the fuck up!" Marcas bellowed. The prince didn't stir. "This is bloody brilliant! I'm stuck in a boat with a dead prince. My ship's gone. And we're drifting away from the stupid island we're supposed to be marooned on!"

There was a small chance that if he kept shouting Gavin might wake up. He hoped he wasn't dead. No matter how ridiculous it seemed now, he felt he might still be able to get a ransom for Gavin, make all of this worth his while.

And if not? He couldn't dwell on it. He already felt like the worst pirate in history.

CHAPTER 7

AT FIRST, GAVIN THOUGHT THE HORRENDOUS POUNDING AT the back of his skull was what woke him, but then he realised it was the shouting. He winced and covered his ears. What in the world was going on? Why was the ship rocking so much? And why was someone kicking his foot?

"Please...stop." Slowly he opened his eyes, and it was terrifyingly clear he was no longer on the *Ebon Drake*. Thunder rumbled in the near distance.

"Thank you! You have no bleeding clue how happy I am you're not dead!" Captain Drake sounded delirious.

Gavin eased himself up to a sitting position and rubbed the back of his head with tender care. There was a nice goose egg there, and likely a nasty bruise to go with it, but otherwise no damage done.

"What's going on?" He looked the captain over with a raised eyebrow. He didn't seem injured from what he could see in the dim light from the lantern settled between them, which was good.

"Quick, come here and untie my hands. We've got to row

to that little island over there before the storm blows our way."

Gavin didn't hesitate to comply. He wasn't in the mood to drown. But once they'd situated themselves in a position where Gavin could faintly see the rope keeping Captain Drake's hands bound together, he realised he had no idea how to undo a knot like that.

"Can I use your sword?"

"I don't care! Just get it done!" the pirate snapped.

"Just remember I'm trying to help you," Gavin said tersely in the captain's ear as he reached around and drew his cutlass. He made quick but careful work of the ropes, only having to cut through one loop before the entire thing came loose.

As soon as he was free to move his arms, Captain Drake put the oars in the oarlocks and got to work rowing them towards the dark blot of land. The sea didn't seem to be preparing for a storm with high winds, and Gavin became hopeful the storm would miss them despite the lightning racing through the clouds and gentle rumbles of thunder. Neither man said anything for what seemed like half an hour, but finally the prince's curiosity got the best of him.

"The last thing I remember was your ill-mannered quartermaster asking me to help him with something, and then something struck the back of my head. What happened?"

"A mutiny, that's what." Drake's face contorted in an ugly scowl. "Guess he's Captain Dawkins now. The bastard."

Gavin sighed and sank down further into the boat. "Obviously. I just don't understand why. Was it our deal?"

"I don't want to talk about it." The pirate looked as if he might start foaming at the mouth.

"Then I'm going to sleep," Gavin drawled.

But he couldn't get comfortable in the tiny area he curled

up in. There would be no stretching out if he didn't want to invade the captain's personal space. Then the little boat began tossing even more, signalling the storm was on their heels.

Eventually, Gavin pushed himself up into a sitting position again. The island loomed behind the captain. He could make out what looked like a forest silhouetted against the dark purple sky.

"I thought we were closer to it when we started..." It still seemed like they had plenty of open water to cover before they reached the little island's beach.

"They're the shoddy pirates; that's what they are," Captain Drake grumbled. "Can't even maroon anyone properly!"

"So they thought you were a shoddy captain?" Gavin said, picking up on the captain's full meaning.

"It's none of your business, Your Highness."

"It might not be, but it looks as though we're going to be stuck enjoying one another's company for a long time, so would it kill you to carry on being civil? Or did they take all your good qualities when they took your ship?"

As soon as the words left his mouth, Gavin regretted saying them. There was no reason for him to pour verbal salt on the man's fresh wound.

"You're lucky I need you or I'd toss your arse overboard!" the captain shouted.

"You *need* me? You must be joking." Gavin crossed his arms over his chest and glowered at the pirate. He wasn't sure why the idea was so laughable. Maybe it was because he'd felt useless on board the *Ebon Drake*. What use could he possibly be on some deserted island?

A clap of thunder drowned out whatever Captain Drake started to say. A flash of lightning illuminated the clouds behind Gavin, but it was bright enough that he could see his pirate companion's face as clear as day for a moment.

"Is there any way to make this thing go faster?" Gavin

said, trying to keep the panic out of his voice even as a gust of wind whipped his hair into his face.

"Not unless you've got an extra pair of oars hidden somewhere on your royal person. Or plans to abandon ship." There was no humour in the captain's words.

Neither of them spoke the rest of the way to shore. Gavin wanted to offer to take over rowing at one point but held his tongue. He wasn't interested in having some pirate mock him for never having rowed a boat before and picking a fine time to learn how.

The little boat threatened to capsize twice before they made it to the shallows of the beach. Captain Drake jumped into waist deep water and began pulling the boat ashore.

"If you're not going to help then you should've just leapt out of the boat," the captain grumbled.

Gavin huffed but got into the water and pushed the boat from behind. The water wasn't cold, but it wasn't exactly warm either. It didn't help that his shoes weren't meant to be slogging through fine sand. He nearly lost his footing several times before they finally had the boat safely out of the water.

Captain Drake took the coil of rope they'd been allowed and tied it to the boat. He dragged it up the beach with Gavin pushing the boat from behind again. It was much slower going now that it was scraping along in the sand, but at least they weren't in danger of drowning anymore.

THE FIRST THING on Marcas's mind was creating some sort of shelter for the night. It didn't have to be permanent, just something to keep them out of the rain. The palm trees just off the beach weren't dense enough to keep them dry on their own, but they found two trees close enough together to allow them to prop the boat up against the trunks, making sure to put the open side downwind. Marcas lashed the boat to the slender palm trunks as best he could with what little rope he had.

"You're sure this won't come crashing down on us while we sleep?" Gavin asked, staring at the makeshift shelter sceptically.

"Afraid to be trapped in a small space with me?" Marcas quipped. Making it to shore had somewhat lightened his mood, at least enough for him to take cheap shots at the prince again. But he was tired and very uninterested in chattering on until sunrise. Another strong gust of wind and the light beginnings of a downpour were all the encouragement his aching muscles needed. After depositing his pistols and cutlass near their other supplies beneath their shelter and snuffing out the lantern, he shrugged his jacket off and folded it into a makeshift pillow and then stretched out on his back under the boat.

It wasn't until the storm shifted to a true rain that Marcas felt Gavin lie down beside him. The prince didn't seem to want to touch any part of him, and for some reason, he found that amusing. He smirked in the dark, knowing it was highly unlikely Gavin could make out his facial expression.

"I won't try anything, if that's what you're afraid of," he said quietly and then yawned. "Too tired anyway."

"That's entirely reassuring." Gavin's tight voice dripped with sarcasm.

"Don't be daft, Gavin. We're both at least half soaked. If we don't huddle together for warmth we'll both catch cold." Marcas wasn't sure his logic was convincing. He was only half-serious. But he found there was nothing wrong with wanting to fall asleep with a warm body alongside his, even if there wasn't a threat of pneumonia.

Just as Marcas began to drift off, he felt Gavin inch closer until he'd pressed up against him.

"This means nothing, Captain Drake," the prince whispered near his ear, barely louder than the rain smacking into the boat above them.

"Of course it's nothing," Marcas mumbled back, pleased with Gavin's use of his title, as if he still commanded the *Ebon Drake*. His chest twisted with a pang of hopelessness, but he ignored it. They'd get off the island. He'd ransom Gavin and buy a new bloody ship if he had to. Whatever it took, he'd be a captain again. "Make sure you forget all about it when you're telling your old man how fearsome and cutthroat I am."

Between the rain pounding against the boat overhead, thunder rumbling intermittently, and Captain Drake's snoring, Gavin couldn't stay asleep. As he tried to rest throughout the night, he found himself missing the hammock he'd grown used to on the *Ebon Drake*. Once sleep finally found him, he had no dreams.

He woke to sunlight warming his face. Then the dull ache at the back of his head caught his attention before he registered Captain Drake's arm wrapped around his middle. The pirate had rolled onto his side in the night and breathed heavily on Gavin's neck. Part of Gavin was thankful the man was no longer snoring, and another part felt outright embarrassed at the sensual signal Drake's every hot breath sent racing down to his groin. The captain wasn't the reason for his morning arousal—that much he was certain of—but his body didn't need any wayward encouragement from the swarthy pirate. Intentional or not. Gavin knew he'd need to extract himself from the captain's embrace as quickly as possible, and without waking him. He didn't want to be regaled with false apologies. It wasn't as if the man had done it on purpose, or so he assumed.

Gavin carefully lifted Drake's fingers up in an attempt to release their grip on his shirt. Thankfully the slight movement made the captain roll onto his back again, taking his arm with him. Gavin didn't care that the snoring started anew as he crawled out from under the boat and brushed as much sand off his skin and clothes as was possible.

He scanned what land he could see for any hints of civilisation. The palm trees obscured much of the area further inland, but there were no docks or buildings to be seen on the stretch of sandy beach. No boats or ships could be seen in the water. They were well and truly marooned.

Gavin began to wonder just how large the island was, whether or not it had some sort of fresh water source and, of course, if there were any carnivorous beasts in residence. He'd heard horrific tales of what sort of creatures lived on secluded, uninhabited islands. Monstrous animals with jaws strong enough to sever bone in one bite. Chimeras, hydras, manticores, and worse still inhabited some of the larger island chains in Siren's Deep's more southerly regions. Gavin had no idea where he and Captain Drake had been stranded in relation to Crakesyde or Highbron, so his imagination began to run wild as he wandered back down to the beach. Part of him wanted to borrow the captain's cutlass and go inland to search for water and something for them to eat, but his internal voice of self-preservation thought it best not to wander off alone.

He squinted up at the sky and noted most of the clouds from the previous night's storm had blown away, leaving a blue expanse marred with little streaks of white behind. It was beautiful. The sky, the sea, the fine sand and the majestic palm trees bowing gracefully along the beach. It was infinitely better to take in nature's beauty in person than to admire man's crude attempts to capture such a scene with paint and canvas. And better to focus on the awe of nature than the deadly forces it often harboured.

His growling stomach forced him away from surveying the relative serenity of the island. He could hear Captain Drake's faint snoring even from the beach. As he wandered back to the boat and the sleeping pirate, he scanned the foliage of all the palm trees he passed, searching for coconuts. There was no way he was going to start the day off with rum if he could help it. Luckily, it looked as though a few of the trees were laden with fruit. Gavin imagined a fresh coconut would taste much better than the dried ones his father imported. *If* he could get one out of a tree, of course.

He peeked under the boat and saw Captain Drake sound asleep, though he'd stopped snoring again. It was no wonder the man was tired, since he'd been the one to row them all the way to shore and done most of the work hauling the boat up the beach, but Gavin needed his help.

"Captain Drake," he said loudly. There was no response. "Captain Drake, it's morning."

The pirate didn't so much as twitch.

"Captain Drake," Gavin said louder. Still nothing. Gavin quirked a brow and watched the pirate for a moment. It was possible he was faking. "Oh look! A ship! We're saved!"

Captain Drake bolted upright. He banged his head on the underside of the boat with a loud *thwack*. Cursing, he rubbed his forehead and glared over at Gavin.

"Now that you're awake, would you mind helping me get some coconuts for our breakfast?" Gavin took a step back as Captain Drake emerged from beneath the shelter and pushed him aside.

"That was far from funny," Captain Drake said. He looked up at the nearest palm trees and pointed to one a few paces away that had four coconuts on it. "Just shake the bloody thing and mind your head."

At first Gavin thought the pirate's comment was genuine concern, but then he remembered that, supposedly, the captain needed him. He couldn't still think it possible to ransom him, could he? So far as Gavin was concerned, one on one was very good odds in his favour if he could secure the cutlass for himself and ensure Captain Drake's pistols were out of reach. Captain Drake was the physically stronger man, but Gavin was an accomplished fencer. All of that was assuming the pirate wouldn't fight dirty…but Gavin held no hope of Drake fighting fair. A non-verbal altercation would have to be avoided at all costs.

"You do realise we're no longer on your ship. You don't have to order me around." Gavin narrowed his eyes at the pirate. It was time to make sure they both understood their place. "In fact, I'd say I should be the one ordering you around if anything. I *am* royalty."

"This?" Captain Drake pointed to the sand emphatically. "Is not Crakesyde."

"So we're agreed. Neither of us has any authority here," Gavin said with a decisive nod.

He walked over to the palm tree and pushed his shoulder against the trunk. It barely shivered, so he tried again. This time he reared back and rammed the tree trunk with his shoulder. Some raindrops that hadn't had the chance to evaporate yet sprinkled down on his head. He glared at Captain Drake.

"Are you really just going to stand there and drink all our rum? I could use your help." Gavin said between attempts to shake the palm tree.

"Our rum?" Drake shoved the cork back in the bottle he'd been drinking from and laughed. "What gives you the idea this isn't every man for himself?"

Gavin took a deep breath, then shot the pirate a bland expression, and crossed his arms over his chest. "Just because neither of us is in charge here doesn't mean we can't work together. You said yesterday that you needed me, and I hope you meant as more than something to cling to while you sleep."

"Cling?" Drake asked, clearly offended at the suggestion.

"Yes. *Cling*. What are you, a parrot?" Gavin was growing annoyed. He abandoned the palm tree and stalked over to the boat again. He took one of the hardtack biscuits out of the little tin they were stashed in. It wasn't going to be a good breakfast, but he was going to eat.

"I don't *cling*," Captain Drake said, giving Gavin a reproving look. "Cuddle, perhaps, but not cling."

Gavin nearly choked on the bit of biscuit he'd bitten off. Crumbs sprayed out of his mouth as he coughed into his free hand. That wasn't what he'd wanted to hear at all! He'd wanted to get a decent jibe in on the captain, but yet again, it was turned around on him.

"You're admitting you did that on purpose then?" Gavin said after he'd cleared his throat. He hoped Captain Drake somehow missed the hot flush of his cheeks and neck.

"And why not? I've told you already I enjoy your company." Captain Drake leaned his back against a palm trunk and uncorked the bottle of rum again. He took a long swig and then smirked at Gavin.

"It isn't appropriate," Gavin said haughtily.

"Why? Because you're a prince and I'm just some scallywag?" The captain laughed again. He made a wide gesture at their surroundings. "Out here we're both no one. You're Gavin, I'm Marcas, and we're both at the same advantages and disadvantages."

"That wasn't what I meant...Marcas," Gavin said, unsure of the use of Captain Drake's given name. It was odd and felt somehow disrespectful. Then again it wasn't as if Marcas called him by his title, and he wasn't sure exactly how much respect he was supposed to have for a man who had kidnapped him and kissed him by force. His face burned twice as hot at the memory. It was wrong, but he'd liked it after the initial confusion and irritation. The press of the pirate's firm lips, the brush of his facial hair, the intensity of the man holding him, wanting him. Gavin cleared his throat. "I only meant that there's a proper way to go about garnering someone's affections if that's what you're after."

It was Marcas's turn to choke. He pounded a fist on his own chest as he coughed and rum dribbled down his goatee and neck. "Garnering…affections!" He spluttered and laughed, wiping his mouth with his sleeve. "You've just made love sound like the most boring business arrangement I've ever heard of."

Gavin was taken aback. His sister constantly told him he had a terrible view of romantic love. Effie tried to read him stories of princesses being swept off their feet by handsome knights or princes into a whirlwind of love. The stories were just that to Gavin: make-believe. The world didn't work that way, after all, at least not for real princes and princesses. He and Effie would both be expected to marry to tie Crakesyde with some other country or newly acquired stretch of land. That was the entire purpose of his setting out for Highbron in the first place. And after marriage? Sure, many courtiers, kings, and queens had lovers if they didn't find passion and love with their spouses, but those relationships were based on lust. So he was especially surprised that a pirate, of all people, seemed to share a fanciful ideal with his little sister. If he weren't so bowled over by the idea, he might have found it amusing.

"Well it is," Gavin finally said. He rolled his eyes when Marcas laughed at him again. "I'm going to try to find a river or a freshwater spring or…something to eat that's closer to the ground than these bloody coconuts."

He stormed off, taking another bite of the horridly bland biscuit as he made his way through the trees and away from Marcas's ridicule. All previous thoughts of striking out on his own being a terrible mistake fled in the face of his ire and embarrassment.

"Gavin! Wait up! I'm coming with you!" Marcas called out, and even though Gavin didn't slow down, mostly to spite the pirate, it didn't take long for Marcas to come running up behind him. He held out one of his pistols to the prince. "Have you ever fired a pistol before? Or any firearm?"

Gavin took the weapon and held it gingerly. He stopped in his tracks and looked from the pistol, which had beautiful silver details and a curling sea serpent down the barrel, to Marcas. Again he was shocked.

"You're sure you want to give this to me after you've just laughed at me?"

"I'm sure you're not a loose cannon," Marcas said. He clapped Gavin on the shoulder in a friendly way. "I'm also sure you've never touched a pistol in your life."

CHAPTER 8

MARCAS HAD BEEN GLAD FOR SO MANY DISTRACTIONS, BUT when most of them disappeared before the day was half gone, his thoughts turned bitter again. They'd discovered a freshwater stream farther inland where the trees grew more dense like a true jungle. There they'd found banana trees interspersed with the coconut palms. They'd gathered a good amount of banana leaves to cover the ground beneath their shelter, and plenty of fruit as well. But Marcas was still in utter disbelief that his crew mutinied, and worst of all, his most trusted crew member had been the driving force behind it all.

The only positive circumstance he could see was that he hadn't been marooned alone. He supposed it was also a good thing his companion was intelligent, good-looking, and obviously attracted to him. It meant he could carry on his game to woo the prince. There wouldn't be anything else to do once they got their campsite in order. Apparently he'd even taken to working on the challenge while asleep. The prince wouldn't last long at all. Especially not with his stodgy views on love.

"You're awfully quiet," Gavin said, his voice interrupting Marcas's thoughts, both the good and the bad.

"I was thinking." He glanced down at the bottle of rum by his hand. It was one of the larger ones he'd had in his cabin, thankfully. That meant more rum now and more capacity for holding water later. It was late afternoon, and he felt the urge to drown his sorrows, just for one night. "Did you want to help me drink the rum?"

"I suppose," Gavin said grudgingly. He abandoned his renewed attempts to shake a few coconuts out of the trees near their shelter.

"I figure we can finish the bottle tonight, and in the morning fill it at the stream like we discussed." He hoped the smile he gave Gavin looked as innocent as he tried to make it appear.

"We do need to have a container to keep water in at camp…and it would be a shame to waste the rum," Gavin admitted. He sat down next to Marcas and put his back against the same tree Marcas leaned against. When Marcas handed over the bottle, Gavin looked down at it. "You do realise this bottle is at least three quarters full?"

"Remember how I said you needed to learn to relax? Now's the perfect time. Just the two of us, complete nobodies stuck on an island in the middle of nowhere. No pretence, no worrying about that social propriety tripe your lot likes to force down each other's throats. Just a beautiful setting, friendly company, and a bottle of rum."

"I think I rather like it here," Gavin remarked and took a long pull from the bottle. He handed it back to Marcas right away and sighed.

"Then why the long face?" Marcas took a deep drink of the rum and made sure to hand the bottle back to Gavin. He wasn't going to let the prince trick him into downing it all by himself.

"There isn't much to do out here but think. Yet everything I think about is rubbish. Excepting my sister of course." Gavin took another drink from the bottle. This time he held on to it.

"I'm in the same boat with you. Which is why we're drinking our sorrows away." Marcas laughed.

They drank in silence for a while, watching the sky turn gold, orange, red, pink, and purple before settling into the deepest of navy blues. The stars twinkled in the darkened sky and were joined by a slice of glowing moon.

"I'm glad it's not winter. I've no idea how to make a fire," Gavin said after handing the bottle back to Marcas. They'd drunk more than half of what had been in the bottle, but they still had a ways to go.

Marcas laughed and set the bottle of rum down beside him. He replaced the cork before returning his gaze to the sky once more. If *he'd* had plenty for the time being, then Gavin had to be three sheets in the wind.

"I'm serious, Marcas," Gavin whined. He leaned over until he leaned on Marcas and poked him in the shoulder. "Why're you always laughing at me anyway? I'm not attempting funny here, Captain."

"Yeah, but you're hilarious," Marcas said with a broad grin. He felt wonderful and wrapped up in the moment, in Gavin leaning against him, resting his head on his shoulder and holding onto his arm.

"I think I had too much to drink," Gavin said. He chuckled into Marcas's shoulder. "Hey, you were right! I am funny!"

"Bet there's loads of things like that you don't know about yourself," Marcas said, his grin turning devilish in the moonlight. He was intoxicated, sure, but he wasn't so drunk he couldn't steer a conversation.

"Oh yeah, like what? If you're so smart…" Gavin laughed

again. He tried to sit up straighter, Marcas guessed, but only succeeded in swaying too far to the right and nearly falling over. He righted himself with a flail of his arms, and Marcas took the opportunity to slide an arm protectively around his new friend's shoulders.

Rum definitely had a way of bringing people closer together. It broke down barriers, had smoothed countless transactions for Marcas in the past, and it never failed to make him a new friend or two.

"Like you've got no balance when you're drunk," Marcas said.

"I knew that." Gavin wrapped his arms around Marcas's middle, presumably to keep from swaying again.

"So you've been drunk before? That's scandalous, Your Highness."

"Oh yeah. Once. I kept flirting with this courtier who my father wanted to marry to my sister… Reginold Dunmire, Duke of Waldren. Older than you. Red hair streaked with stately white. And his arse…" Gavin trailed off and ducked his chin, as if he realised he'd been too candid. But then he looked up at Marcas, brows furrowed. "Drinking makes me lecherous."

"Happens to the best of us." Marcas found it funny that even after declaring such a statement, Gavin didn't let go of him. In fact, he'd begun trailing his fingers up and down Marcas's side.

"I wish we had more rum."

"You've had enough for tonight. We both have. Promise," Marcas said and let his own hand run over Gavin's arm. Sitting there together, holding one another, was wonderful. He hated to be the voice of reason, but neither one of them could afford to throw up what little they'd eaten that day. A little headache the next day would be payment enough for having drunk so much.

"We should've played a drinking game. Pirates know all sorts of drinking games, right?" Gavin rested his head against Marcas's chest as he spoke.

"We can play one tomorrow." Marcas laughed lightly again as he thought of a few choice drinking games, ones a sober Gavin might not consent to play. He peered down at Gavin and resisted the urge to run his fingers through the prince's loose hair, barely illuminated in the moonlight.

A huge yawn made Gavin shudder and then sigh in annoyance. "I think I should lie down."

"C'mon, it's just a few yards to the boat."

Marcas reluctantly let Gavin release him and used the tree to assist his standing up. Once he felt stable enough to help him, he pulled Gavin to his feet and they trudged to their shelter.

"I like this drowning sorrows. We should build a house and never go back to the rest of the world. The island's beautiful and carefree," Gavin announced, slurring half his words. He crawled under the boat shelter and readjusted Marcas's coat into a better pillow before settling down on their banana leaves.

Marcas smiled in amusement. The stuffy, worrywart prince had finally let go of his troubles, at least for one night. He crawled under the boat as well and lay down on his side, using Gavin's coat for his pillow this time. As much as he wanted to pull Gavin to him and do all manner of improper things to him, Marcas didn't want to take advantage of his friend's inebriated state. If he wanted to truly win Gavin over, he knew he'd have to continue to be a gentleman. No more impulsive kisses, that was for damn sure. Not unless he was clear Gavin was interested.

Suddenly Gavin scooted over and pressed his body flush against Marcas, running his hand over the pirate's shoulder and neck and then tangling his fingers in Marcas's short hair.

Gavin's lips found the other man's cheek first and then fumbled down to meet his mouth. If Gavin wanted to give in to his obvious desires—the way he devoured Marcas with his eyes at every opportunity had spoken volumes from day one—Marcas wouldn't turn him away. Even if he probably should.

The kisses were sloppy, wanton, and Marcas enjoyed every single one. He pulled Gavin closer and rubbed his back, wishing there wasn't a shirt in his way, but wanting to let Gavin take the lead. Gavin wedged his hand between them to awkwardly caress the hardness Marcas had been pressing against Gavin's hip. Marcas could tell Gavin seemed unsure of what he was doing, but he attributed all fumbling to the rum.

"I've only done this once before," Gavin whispered between kisses. He fumbled to unfasten Marcas's belt buckle, then the buttons on his pants.

"Done what?" Marcas breathed.

Gavin's soft hand stroked his erection in answer, unhindered by troublesome clothing. Marcas bucked his hips; then Gavin's hand disappeared. But before Marcas could fully vocalise a protest, Gavin shoved him onto his back. Gavin shifted positions, and then the warm, wet silkiness of tongue ran over Marcas's cock.

Marcas put a hand on Gavin's head, eager to touch any part of him, but only being able to run his fingers through his hair. How could he say no when Gavin was so eager? He bit back a loud sigh as Gavin's mouth engulfed him, and struggled not to jerk his hips to urge Gavin to move faster. Gavin's mouth slid up and down his cock at a maddeningly slow pace. But as soon as Gavin gently caressed Marcas's balls, he lost it and gasped out some unintelligible sound while he came.

Without a word, Gavin refastened Marcas's pants and

belt buckle and then curled up beside him, arm slung over the pirate's chest.

"You...are bloody amazing," Marcas whispered, still feeling wonderfully relaxed after such a release. It had been too long since he'd taken pleasure in anything but his own hand. His cautiousness had cost him the luxury of hiring a good whore, and it had been more than a handful of years since he'd dallied with a man due to mutual attraction alone.

He shifted onto his side and kissed Gavin, who seemed to have gone back to being less than relaxed. It was no matter to Marcas; he wanted to return the favour. It was the gentlemanly thing to do, considering the circumstances, and he couldn't deny how much he wanted to taste the prince.

"I think I drank too much," Gavin whispered back, turning his face away to avoid yawning in Marcas's face.

"You seem fine to me," Marcas said. He let his hands roam over Gavin's torso, then down to the front of his breeches. There was no question Gavin was only at half mast, which was likely the source of his change of demeanour. Too much rum could hinder amorous advances, but only if you let it.

Gavin didn't stop Marcas from unbuttoning his pants or exploring any part of his body. After a few gentle strokes, Gavin's cock rose to full attention in Marcas's hand, and the sloppy kisses started again.

"Please don't stop," Gavin mumbled against his lips. His hips bucked wildly against Marcas's fist. One foot crooked behind his leg, giving Gavin's thrusts better leverage.

It took some time, and a change of positions, but Gavin finally found his quiet release. Marcas felt more contented with Gavin's languid body in his arms and the man's happy sigh against his ear than he had since well before the Crimson Queen had put him on the run.

THE LIGHT FILTERING through Gavin's eyelids made him roll over onto his side. His head pounded, and he massaged his temples, but it didn't help. All he could think about was how thirsty and hungry he was, and how he would never drink rum ever again.

He sat up, careful not to smack his head into the underside of the boat, and hugged his knees for a moment. He'd just begun to drift back to sleep when he realised he wasn't wearing his shirt. A quick look around and Gavin found it balled up near his feet. Memories of what he'd done the night before came flooding back to him.

"Bloody hell," he cursed. He'd never be able to look at Marcas the same way again!

There was no arguing with himself over what had possessed him to do that. He could blame the rum all day long, but he knew that had only helped him to feel bold enough to act on his existing desires. It was something his short-lived relationship with his stable hand had taught him. He knew he'd wanted it to happen—he'd wanted to lay hands on the man since he'd laid eyes on him. Ever since that first kiss, when he'd been a prisoner, Gavin had forced himself to ignore any sort of sexual attraction he'd felt towards Marcas with little success. There was likely something wrong with him that he could forgive such a transgression as that ill-won kiss in the face of his own ridiculous attraction. But berating himself and trying to bottle up his desires hadn't been much use. He'd been transparent. He hadn't even tried to convince the man he was interested in women. And keeping his feelings locked away, under pressure, had only contributed to the ease with which he'd indulged himself the night before.

Things truly were different on the island. They were friends of a sort, but mostly due to circumstance. There was no hope of Marcas's ransom plan working while they were stuck on the island, and if they ever managed to make it off the island, that grand plan would be just as difficult to execute. Which meant they were truly on equal ground, and Gavin couldn't use Marcas's being his captor as an excuse to ignore his desires.

Something smacked against the hull of the boat and sent Gavin's headache into more painful territory. He crawled out from under it, dragging his shirt with him, and squinted against the bright sunlight.

"What in the world is going on?" he asked, looking around for Marcas, who appeared behind the boat shelter and held up two coconuts, a huge grin on his face.

"Sorry about that, it hit the boat when it fell." Marcas came around to the front of their shelter and handed Gavin one of the coconuts.

Still reeling from his headache, Gavin stood there and looked down at the coconut with a bewildered expression while Marcas took the cutlass to the other one. The sword wasn't meant for hacking open fruit, but it seemed to be going well. However, Gavin didn't feel he could handle much more of the loud noise Marcas made in the process.

"Sleep well?" Marcas asked after he'd managed to split the first coconut. He traded it for the one Gavin held and set about trying to hack the second one open. "You look a bit green this morning."

"I uh...yes. Just...have a headache is all," Gavin said quietly, not wanting to add to the noise. He took a sip from the coconut, glad all the milk hadn't spilled out. It was strange how he felt a sudden need for utensils and dishes. He tried scraping some of the meat of the coconut out with his fingers but didn't have any luck. "Do you still have that knife?"

"Hang on..." A moment later the second coconut had been successfully cleaved. Then Marcas reached into his boot and pulled out a knife with a small blade. He cut a chunk out of his own coconut for himself and handed the knife to Gavin. Breakfast carried on in relative silence, and Gavin found he had trouble looking at Marcas at all, even as they traded the knife back and forth. Every time he did sneak a glance at the pirate, he saw a pleased smirk on the man's face.

A part of Gavin hoped Marcas wasn't going to expect a repeat of the previous night's debauchery. The other part of him was happy to recall just how amazing the pirate's rough hands felt on his skin, how his cock had felt in his mouth. Gavin set what was left of his coconut on the ground between his feet and put his aching head in his hands. How could he be thinking of carnal pleasures when he should be worrying about how they were going to survive for more than a few days?

"How long do you think we can live off fruit and rum?" he asked, sounding miserable even to his own ears.

"Not sure. What? Two days and you're tired of it already? Just last night you said you wanted to stay here forever," Marcas said, stifling a laugh by shoving a chunk of coconut meat in his mouth.

"No one knows I'm missing yet. Your crew turned on you. So I guess I'll get my wish since no one's even trying to rescue us." Gavin got up and stalked off towards the stream, taking his shirt with him. Bathing might help clear his head, and he needed to at least rinse his shirt so he could wear it again. He could already feel the pale skin on his shoulders and arms burning in the morning sun.

CHAPTER 9

THE CRIMSON QUEEN STRUCK THE OLD PIRATE'S BACK WITH the cat o' nine tails. She hoped each successive lash would rip his flesh from his bones. There was blood, so much delightful blood, running down his back in rivulets. It flew off the cat in a spray as she swung it again and again.

"Where is he!?" she screeched like a banshee.

Finally, she decided she'd had enough of asking the same question over and over again. She handed the cat to Arreid and bent over the bleeding pirate tied to the main mast. The queen pressed herself against his backside so firmly it was obscene. The pirate whimpered at the contact to his ruined back.

"Don't know…Your Highness," he breathed, taking what strength he had left to force the words out.

"Mr. Dawkins, if you don't conjure up the coordinates of the island where you decided to maroon Captain Drake, understand I'll have you keelhauled. The *Ebon Drake* misses its captain, Mr. Dawkins, and you will pay the price for forcing yourself upon it. *With your blood*," she whispered in his ear, just for him. A private conversation.

"It was some island back north of here! I told you! We left there maybe…two or three days ago!" Mr. Dawkins cried out with renewed strength of will.

"We wanted to join you, Yer Majesty!" the cabin boy called out from across the deck. He was held, with some other choice members of the crew, by the queen's crew. The rest had been locked below deck.

His statement caught her by surprise, but instead of leaving the *Ebon Drake*'s quartermaster alone, she grabbed him by his scraggly, greying ponytail and wrenched his head back from the mast.

"Is that true, Mr. Dawkins? You wanted to join me?" she demanded.

"Yes. Yes, 'tis true," he forced out.

"And the rest of the crew?" she asked, a sweet smile brightening her face.

"Yes, them too. 'Tis true!"

"Lies! You're just as lily-livered now as you were when you sailed under Deadeye Angus Drake, you old traitor!" the queen bellowed in her high voice, causing everyone on board to wince. She released her grip on his hair and walked over to the cabin boy. "Arreid, darling, Mr. Dawkins is ready to become much more intimate with the *Ebon Drake*. Prepare him."

"Aye, My Queen," Arreid said and began untying the queen's victim from the main mast.

"You, boy, what's your name?" the queen commanded lightly of Captain Drake's former cabin boy. She lifted his chin with her index finger and went about inspecting him as if he were some piece of merchandise.

"Alan M-Morris, Yer M-majesty," he said, his voice cracking more than once as he spoke.

"Alan, did you really want to join my crew as you said?" She stroked his tanned cheek.

He nodded, closing his eyes at her touch. The queen imagined his expression conveyed appreciation for her kind display of affection, but it could just as easily have been out of fear. Both thoughts pleased her.

"I'd be greatly honoured, Yer Highness."

The Crimson Queen clapped excitedly and ordered the cabin boy be released from his bonds. Once freed, she hugged him tight, pleased he returned the warm sentiment despite the blood covering her.

"I've been needing a new cabin boy!" she said, hooking her arm through his and escorting him across a gangplank to her own ship. "The last one had a jealous streak and tried to kill Arreid in his sleep, so I had to string him up from the nearest yardarm and slit his throat. Now, do you know how to read and write? You'll have to sign my articles of agreement before you're really part of my crew. Don't look so nervous! I'll read them out loud to you if you can't read."

The next few days were strained with Gavin only speaking when he was spoken to. It drove Marcas crazy. He tried to find other things to do besides attempting to carry on a conversation with Gavin, like starting a fire. Most of the pieces of wood and bark he'd found were still damp from another evening rain, and all his best efforts produced minimal amounts of smoke. Eventually he gave up.

"What's on your mind, Gavin?" He'd walked down to the beach where Gavin skipped shells and small rocks across the water.

"Too many things, really." His tone made it clear he wanted to be left alone.

Marcas, however, was tired of spending the day by himself.

The sun neared the horizon, and he wasn't about to spend the night alone either. He wouldn't put it past Gavin to find somewhere else to sleep or ask him to. He just wasn't sure why. The rum had pushed Gavin's inhibitions aside, but he'd still been the one to make all the first moves. That had to count for something.

"Anything you want to share?"

"Nothing you'd understand," Gavin said and lobbed another shell at the sea. He looked around for something else to throw in the water.

"Because I'm not a prince or because I'm a pirate?" Marcas tried not to take offense. Gavin was in a difficult place in life, and Marcas could appreciate that. He was far away from the only home he'd ever known and knew there was a great chance he'd never be able to go back. "I think we're a lot more alike than you think."

Gavin snorted derisively. He bent down, picked up a fragment of a larger shell, and inspected it for a moment. "You're a thief and a liar, Marcas. I believe the only thing we have in common, besides being stuck on this island, is that we're both men. There the similarities end."

"You're absolutely right, *Mr. Smith*," Marcas said. He sat down on the sand and enjoyed the ocean view with what daylight there was left.

"That was my father's idea," Gavin said defensively.

"But you were the one to carry it out." Marcas shrugged and flashed Gavin a smirk.

"It was a direct order from the king!" Gavin stood and deliberately turned his back on Marcas.

"That's no excuse. Just an explanation," Marcas said. He pulled a half-buried shell out of the sand and flung it over towards Gavin's feet.

Gavin glanced down at the shell but chose to ignore it. Instead he crossed his arms over his chest, looking every bit the teenager. "You really are a terrible pirate. What sort of pirate is so bloody friendly to his captive?"

It was Marcas's turn to get defensive. "A pirate's got to have friends, just the same as anyone else. If you want to play prisoner again so badly, all you have to do is say the word."

"Just because I'm not tied up or locked away doesn't mean you're not still considering selling me back to my family." Gavin turned and faced Marcas again, a hard look on his features.

"You really are thickheaded, Gavin," Marcas shook his head in mild disbelief. *Something* was eating Gavin up inside, and it probably had to do with trying to come to terms with never seeing his sister again. Or dying on some island with only a pirate for a companion. He was going to be unbearable to live with if he didn't settle his emotional problems, and fast. "But I'll say it again: I like you, and we're on even ground here. I can't ransom you now, even if I still wanted to. Why is all that so hard to believe?"

"What's the point of us being friends now when I'll be expected to hang you later?" Gavin let his arms fall back to his sides and walked back towards their shelter.

"I thought we'd decided no one was going to rescue us?" Marcas called back over his shoulder. So that was the source of it: Marcas was a pirate and Gavin was a future king. It didn't strike Marcas as a problem.

He sat on the beach for a little while longer before heading back to camp himself. When he got there, he was surprised to see Gavin struggling to undo the knots in the rope that secured the boat against the trees.

"Going to row home?" Marcas asked.

"I'm tired of standing around here. I thought it might be a good idea to see how big the island is. Maybe there's a sign of civilisation elsewhere, and rowing will be faster than exploring the island on foot." Gavin ran a hand through his hair and went back to trying to figure out the rope knots.

Marcas walked over to Gavin and put a hand on his shoulder. He tried to get Gavin to look at him, but he kept his head down even though he'd given up on the rope.

"I'm sorry for the way I acted when I was drunk. It was the exact opposite of proper behaviour, and I'm afraid I've given you the wrong idea," Gavin said quietly.

"The idea that you're attracted to me?" Marcas couldn't hide his smirk. That might have been the only idea he had right about the tormented young man.

"No." Gavin rolled his eyes. "The idea that I'm easy and only interested in sex."

Marcas laughed, he couldn't help it. Even knowing it would probably make Gavin more distant didn't stop him from expressing his amusement. "You were drunk!"

Gavin became stony-faced again, unmoved by the pirate's mirth. "Now *you're* making up excuses for my actions. That's brilliant."

"Gavin, I'll be honest with you." Marcas laughed again when Gavin narrowed his eyes at him. "I wouldn't mind if something like the other night happened again. That doesn't mean I expect it to."

"I liked that we were becoming friends despite our outlandish circumstances. Now it feels like my impropriety has ruined even that."

"Only because you're so bloody stubborn," Marcas said. He looked around, suddenly aware of the change in light. The sun was setting, which meant any trek around the island would be best saved for the next day. "There's no rule here on this island that says we can't be friends and attracted to one another."

"So you believe we're stuck here for the rest of our lives?"

Gavin asked. His shoulders sagged then, his annoyance clearly turning to sadness at some loss of hope.

"I won't get anywhere idly hoping some ship's going to show up and save us from ourselves. And neither will you."

Marcas put his arm around Gavin's shoulders and steered him over to their pile of food. The hard tack biscuits were nearly gone, meaning they'd have to find some other source of food besides fruit. So long as the weather held out for another day, they could build a fire to cook with. They'd both seen a few crabs on the beach, and there were bound to be fish somewhere around the island. How they'd catch the fish would be another matter, but he was sure they were both clever enough to come up with something.

CHAPTER 10

When Gavin woke up the next morning, he felt somewhat better about what life had recently handed him. Aside from being hungry and missing Effie and the comforts of home, he wasn't doing badly for himself, and he thought as he listened to Marcas's light snoring, he had one of the most interesting companions. This was the adventure of a lifetime. How many times had he begged his father to let him travel abroad? How often had he asked his father to let him see the world before he had too many responsibilities to be able to do so?

He'd finally got his wish. It wasn't exactly what he'd hoped for, but it had been exciting. He was happy to leave the overabundance of misgivings from the previous day behind him. Marcas had been right. There was no reason to structure his life around whether or not they were going to be rescued. There would be nothing wrong with living for the moment so long as they were stranded. Meaning he wouldn't let himself worry about future consequences of befriending a pirate.

Gavin was also not allowing himself to indulge in finding

a reason to ignore his feelings for Marcas, platonic or otherwise. It was much easier to write it off as stemming from his having had very few friendships.

He rolled over and watched Marcas sleep for a little while longer. He'd never had to share sleeping space with anyone before. It was a lot more comforting than he'd anticipated, but he thought maybe he craved a little security since they were out in the open. All the same, Gavin could have done without the snoring and waking up occasionally to Marcas cuddling him. It might have been a drunken idea, but building some sort of house was starting to seem like a wonderful plan. Unfortunately, Gavin didn't know the first thing about construction, and they were woefully lacking in tools.

"Looks like you're happier today," Marcas mumbled and then yawned. He smirked at Gavin and watched him through half-lidded eyes.

"I'm excited about getting out there and finding out how large the island is, I guess." Gavin smiled at him.

They both crawled out from under their shelter and stretched.

"I've been to some of these islands before, and they're all fairly small. No signs of human civilisation on them," Marcas said as he untied the knots securing the boat to the trees. He coiled the rope and looped it over his shoulder, instructing Gavin on how to help him carry the boat down to the beach while they were under it. It was much easier than dragging it down to the water.

After a quick breakfast, they set out in the boat. Gavin took to pointing out colourful fish and sea birds. It was like he was seeing everything for the first time, even though they'd been on the island for a few days.

"We have to figure out a way to catch some fish," Gavin

said. "We could take some thread from my coat to make a line. I'm not sure what we could use for a hook though."

"Or bait," Marcas said, but he was smiling at the idea.

"I'll bet crab meat would work. That is if we could catch one. They're awfully fast." His mind was going now, and he could see it all perfectly in his head. The only real missing piece was the hook. He doubted whittling one out of wood would work. If it was a strong fish it might just snap the end of the hook and swim off with the bait.

"I'd rather eat the crab than feed it to the fish." Marcas raised a brow at Gavin. "Oh and you *are* planning to take a turn rowing today, yeah?"

"Well, yes, of course. It doesn't look that difficult," Gavin said with a smile and a nod. He felt he was coordinated enough to row them around the coast of the island.

As they continued rowing along the coastline, it became obvious the island looked to be about as big as Gavin had guessed. There were still no signs of human inhabitants, and they were already a quarter of the way around the landmass. Judging by the position of the sun compared to when they'd set out, an hour couldn't have gone by yet.

"We should have brought something for lunch," Gavin said.

"I hope you're not as sick of bananas as I am." Marcas sighed.

They both looked over at the landscape of the island. It was much more lush than the area near their camp, and the beach was smaller, surrounded by rocks covered in algae, barnacles, and shrivelled strands of seaweed.

"I'll find something to use as a hook once we're back at camp and we can go fishing." Gavin felt very confident suddenly, and he wasn't sure why. It might have been the mere prospect of having something filling to eat for a change.

They found a suitable spot to pull ashore and had a lunch of oranges and bananas. Gavin made sure to collect as many oranges as he could reach and put them in the boat for later. At least it would give them a little variety for the next couple of days.

Then it was Gavin's turn to row the boat. Marcas made quite a show of being able to relax in the little craft and doled out some advice on how to better control the direction of the boat with the oars. Gavin got the hang of it quickly, but they moved much slower than when Marcas had been rowing.

"I like this. Reminds me of home," Marcas said. He seemed humoured instead of bitter, and Gavin was glad for that.

"I'm sorry about your ship. It was your father's, wasn't it?" Even though he knew it was ridiculous, Gavin couldn't shake the notion that he was somehow responsible for the crew deciding to mutiny. Marcas had been right to be concerned about their obsessive superstitions, and it was obvious their fear of Gavin's hair colour cancelled out all plans to ransom him. He was sure it would have been different if they'd had any idea who he really was. Marcas had kept his word on keeping his identity a secret. It was something to truly be grateful for, no matter what the pirate's initial motives for keeping the secret might have been.

Marcas nodded. His eyes turned to the waters of Siren's Deep glistening under the sun.

"If we are rescued, and I know it's unlikely, but if we are, I'll do what I can to return the *Ebon Drake* to you. And if that's not possible, I can get you a new ship." Gavin wasn't sure how long any of that would take, but he was confident he could pull some strings without his father noticing.

"If I can't captain the *Ebon Drake*, I might as well go into extremely early retirement." Marcas sighed and shrugged. "Then history will remember me as the pirate who gave up.

Which means I either stay here and let the world think I've died a dramatic death by wasting away, or I find a way to hunt down Dawkins and slit him from starboard to larboard before he can open his weaselling mouth."

Gavin swallowed hard at the mental image that produced. He had no kind thoughts for Mr. Dawkins, but envisioning anyone being cut open disturbed him.

"It's a better end than he deserves," Marcas added when he saw Gavin's reaction to his harsh words.

"I'm not going to disagree," Gavin said.

By the time they'd nearly completed their circuit and sighted their beach, it was just past noon. Gavin felt like his shoulders would never be the same, and he wondered if the feeling of his arms hanging on by fragile, aching threads would ever go away.

Then his heart leapt into his throat. He blinked once, twice, unsure if he could trust his eyes, but there it was, plain as the palms scattered across their beach.

"Marcas, it's a ship!"

This was it! The moment they'd been waiting for!

CHAPTER 11

THE MOMENT MARCAS DRAKE HAD BEEN DREADING FOR THREE years had finally caught up with him. And, instead of handling the situation like a rational man who could take care of himself in any situation, he panicked.

"Back! We need to go back the other way!" he hissed at Gavin and motioned frantically with both hands. He'd caught the increase in rowing speed as soon as Gavin had laid eyes on the ship, but one glance over his shoulder at those blood-red sails told Marcas they needed to be picking up speed in the opposite direction.

"Whatever for? Marcas, this is our ticket off this ruddy island!" Gavin protested, but at least he'd stopped rowing.

"It's a one-way ticket to ridicule and embarrassment for me. Possibly a one-way ticket to the bottom of the Deep for you. Or she might try to ransom you. Of course, she doesn't know who you are, but your clothes… And how the fuck did she find me?"

"You've just gone mad, haven't you?" Gavin said dryly, eyes half-lidded in irritation.

"Please, Gavin, just…row back round the island. Or let

me! Just hurry!" Marcas pleaded. This was a desperate time, and he was now very determined to get as far away from the *Crimson Wake* as possible. He wondered how it could have happened. He'd been so careful for so long! Someone must have sold him out. Either that or she'd found the *Ebon Drake*, and his old crew had let their tongues wag to appease the queen.

"Why are you…?" Gavin began, but then his eyes went wide. "Red sails… That's the Crimson Queen's ship, isn't it?"

Marcas nodded. Without saying another word, Gavin handed the oars over. Marcas rowed as if his life depended on it, and the huge hulk of a ship began to diminish behind them.

"What are we going to do? They're going to find the lantern and our coats if they do any searching at all. They'll know someone's here," Gavin said quietly, as if his voice might carry all the way back to the ship.

"We'll hide out at the back of the island for as long as we can. Hope they give up and go away." Marcas hated how strained his voice sounded, but there was no time to cover up fear with false confidence. "She's looking for me, so they won't stop searching until they've covered every inch of the island."

"Are you rivals? My father said you've both been terrorizing some of the newer colonies. I mean, 'terrorizing' may be a strong—"

"No offense taken. That's my job. I'm proud of my accomplishments. And I suppose we're sort of rivals, but I've been avoiding her for years now. She's bound to be pissed she hasn't been able to check up on me," Marcas said.

"I…I think we've been spotted." Gavin pointed a shaky finger over Marcas's shoulder. "There're two boats coming this way!"

"Shit!" Marcas pushed his arms to row faster, but there

was only so much he could do before his muscles began to protest. He gritted his teeth and concentrated on the rhythm of the oars.

If they were caught, he had no idea how he'd weasel his way out of the queen's insane grasp. She'd become completely psychotic, and while he wasn't afraid of coming to harm under her sword, he was terrified at the very real prospect of being stuck sailing with her for an indefinite amount of time. There was a chance she might help him recover the *Ebon Drake*, but it was more likely she'd laugh in his face for having lost the bloody thing.

"They're gaining on us!" Gavin said. "How is that possible?"

"Probably have more than one person rowing," Marcas ground out. He wouldn't admit defeat yet.

They swerved into a little inlet and then scrambled to drag the boat up the beach and hide it behind one of the larger rocks. Marcas started for the trees, which were dense, but Gavin grabbed his arm before he could take more than a few steps.

"What about the huge mark we just left in the sand?" he said, pointing at their footprints and the drag mark from the boat.

"We don't have time to worry about that." Marcas shook Gavin's hand off his arm and gestured for him to follow him into the trees.

They ran as fast as they could while dodging tree trunks and attempting not to trip over undergrowth and vines. Marcas stopped to catch his breath. They had a good head start, but it was time to wait and listen. He leaned his back up against a large palm tree and pulled Gavin to him.

"If we stay here, they won't be able to see us just by looking through the trees," he whispered.

"Why don't we climb a tree?" Gavin whispered back. "Or we could hide under some of those fallen leaves?"

"It might make too much noise. We don't want to draw attention if they've come ashore."

Despite the dangerous situation they were in, Marcas fought the urge to kiss Gavin. They were so close, breath mingling, hearts pounding out a rapid beat under clammy skin and sweat-damp clothing. And if he were being honest with himself about their chances of getting away, it might be the last time they were able to be so near one another. He took a pistol from its place on the strap slung diagonally over his chest and handed it to Gavin.

"I've no idea how to use this thing," Gavin whispered.

He was nervous; Marcas could see it in his eyes.

"Doesn't matter. Having one is better than looking unarmed."

Minutes crept by as they stood there, anticipating the worst, listening to the sounds of the forest. Birds twittered and called to one another, and the ocean's waves could still be heard.

"What if she—"

But Gavin's words were cut short by Marcas's fingers on his lips. The sound of footsteps on leaf litter reached both their ears. A few birds fluttered away from their roosts nearby, and Marcas hoped it wouldn't draw undue attention to their location. He pulled his second pistol out of its holster as carefully and quietly as possible. He wouldn't take the chance of cocking it, since the sound of something metal would carry.

All they could do was hope the queen's men would give up and go back to their ship. Yet the sound of people walking through the forest grew louder as the pirates came closer.

"They've gotta be here somewheres, mate," a rough,

female voice said. She sounded far too close for Marcas's liking, but she wasn't the queen.

"Search the tree tops. Captain Drake might try being clever," a cool voice replied. A very familiar voice: Arreid, the Crimson Queen's lapdog of a first mate. She'd rescued him after he'd been exiled from Aesgill for murder and set adrift in the Deep. He was every bit as cruel-hearted as the queen herself, and blindly loyal to her.

Gavin grabbed Marcas's hand, and he could feel the prince shaking with fear. Stories of the Crimson Queen's exploits had circulated far and wide—it was no wonder he was scared. He had every right to be. Most tales of the queen's dark deeds didn't have to be embellished in the retelling; they were evil enough on their own. The look in Gavin's eyes showed his inner strength at work, keeping him silent and rooted in place.

Everything had gone too quiet. The voices had stopped, and the crunching of leaves and forest debris had ceased.

"Drop your weapons," Arreid said as he stepped around the side of the tree they were hidden behind. His rapier pointed at Marcas's chest.

Gavin's grip on his hand tightened, and he took half a step back.

"Yours first," Marcas said, attempting to sound casual. He was glad his voice wasn't shaky, and he took the opportunity to give Gavin's hand a reassuring squeeze. At the same time, if he held Gavin in place he could ensure the man didn't bolt. Any sudden moves would likely get him shot.

"We have you surrounded," Arreid said, his voice cool and emotionless.

"And if we don't feel like being unarmed with your sword shoved in our faces?" Marcas asked.

Arreid shifted his sword to point the sharp tip at Gavin's

neck. "We were only ordered to bring *you* unharmed, Captain Drake."

Marcas dropped his pistol to the forest floor and heard Gavin do the same.

∽

THE CRIMSON QUEEN shook the sand off Marcas's coat and held it up with a grin. Then she hugged it tightly as if it were the man himself.

"Ooh, Marcas! Finally!" she said into the fabric.

"Erm…Yer Majesty?" Morris said, and the Crimson Queen looked over at him. "It's his coat."

"And? It means he's here. It means it's only a matter of time before Arreid brings him back to me," she said, agitated. What was the boy implying? That she was daft? That she didn't know the difference between a person and an article of clothing? But then she remembered what a great help the boy had been, and her temper cooled. She grinned at her cabin boy and giggled. "It's all thanks to you for recognizing the island!"

"Oh, that was nothin', Yer Highness," Morris said, flushing. His modesty was terribly endearing to the queen.

"Nonsense, my dear boy!" She handed him the coat and gestured for him to go below deck. "I want you to take a brush to this. Make sure there's no sand left anywhere on it, and let me know if you find anything interesting in the pockets."

Morris nodded and hurried off to do his captain's bidding.

The queen paced across the main deck of her ship with a smile plastered on her face. Today was an excellent day, and she was pleased when she only had to wait an hour more before the two boats sent off to fetch Captain Drake and his little friend were spotted again. She dashed over to the railing and peered through her spyglass. The crew members were easily recognised, and in the boat rowed by her darling Arreid was a redheaded male—that must have been Mr. Smith—and Marcas Drake. Her shriek of delight caught even her by surprise, and she laughed to herself in embarrassment.

"Morris, have that coat ready in ten minutes!" she shouted at the top of her lungs.

The sun met the horizon by the time the boat crews returned, but the queen didn't need bright light to recognise Marcas, brought stumbling on deck with his hands tied behind his back. She ran over to him and pulled him into a tight embrace.

"My darling baby brother!" She kissed him on the cheek and then went back to hugging him.

"Rhona, you're crushing," Marcas gasped out.

"Oh! Sorry! Don't know my own strength." She released him, crooked her arm through his, and turned him around to face Gavin. For some reason he looked familiar to her, but she couldn't quite place what it was about his face that sparked a hint of recognition. It might have been the hair or perhaps his long nose. She hadn't met many redheaded men before, most likely because of the ridiculous superstition about redheads and sailing ships. "And who's your surprised looking friend? He's nearly as handsome as you are."

"Mr. Smith," Marcas replied.

"C'mon, brother dear, you've been marooned with Mr. Smith for days now. If I know you at all, you're on a first name basis," Rhona said with a sly grin. It had always been a point of amusement that her brother preferred men. It was absurdly ironic in her book that anyone so attractive and charming should be granted the bad luck of a narrowed choice in partners. She felt immense relief that her own attractions were varied.

"Gavin Smith, this is my sister Rhona Drake," Marcas said, sounding rather defeated.

"You can call me 'Your Highness' or 'Your Majesty' if you don't mind," she said to Gavin. "And it's thirty lashes if you do."

The horrified look on the man's face was priceless. Rhona laughed and gestured for Arreid to take the redhead below deck. She escorted her brother to her cabin, and once they were inside, she sat him in one of her newest upholstered chairs: red fabric with an Aesgillian fairy motif on a cherry-wood frame. She'd acquired them as plunder in a recent razing, and they'd quickly become two of her favourite pieces of furniture. That they reminded Arreid of his childhood home and his mother, who'd been a talented weaver, meant more to Rhona than how lovely and comfortable they were.

"It's been far too long, Marcas," she said and sat on his lap. She draped an arm around his shoulders and pressed her cheek to his forehead, needing to feel how solid he was, how real and warm. "Morris tells me you've been avoiding me on purpose. I slapped him for the mere suggestion! Tell me it's not true, darling."

"Rhona, why in the world would I spend three years avoiding the only family I've got left?"

"That's exactly what I thought!" She hummed to herself, satisfied with his answer. Even if he was lying, she'd take his word as truth. She only ever wanted to spend time with her brother and make sure he was faring well. The rumours she'd heard hadn't been good, and it was obvious from his crew's mutiny that things were even worse than anyone outside the *Ebon Drake* could have known.

"Wait...Morris? My cabin boy's here?" Marcas's eyes went wide, and he smiled.

"*My* cabin boy," Rhona corrected.

"*Your* cabin boy?" Marcas's face screwed up as he tried puzzling out how that had happened, but confusion quickly turned to delight. "So you've already recovered my ship! What of the rest of my mutinous crew? Did you keelhaul the lot of them?"

"They had to be punished; I'm so glad you understand, Marcas. You and Arreid are the only ones who truly understand me. Of course, Daddy did...but he's not here to be proud of his princess," she said and hugged Marcas again. She'd missed him so much. She was grateful to be able to hug her own flesh and blood. While Arreid understood her and comforted her whenever she needed it, he wasn't big on hugging. "I keelhauled Dawkins after his back met my cat. Then I burned the *Ebon Drake* with the crew inside."

"You *what?!*" Marcas bellowed.

Rhona covered her ear and made a sound of disapproval. She hopped up off his lap, thinking it would be a good idea to pour her brother some rum. He'd need it if he was going to handle the loss of his ship.

"Marcas, I had to. You of all people should understand."

"I'm having a little trouble understanding why the fuck you set fire to my bloody home!" The anguish was evident in his voice, and Rhona had a secret hope that he wouldn't cry. It wouldn't do at all, but he was so overemotional sometimes.

"It was tainted. Daddy always said the *Ebon Drake* should never be captained by anyone whose name isn't Drake. You know that." Rhona walked back over to her brother with a glass of rum in hand. She tilted it up to his lips slowly and offered him a kind smile. "Here, drink up, me hearty."

Marcas complied readily, as she'd expected. He was never

one to turn down his favourite drink, though she was surprised when he downed the entire glass in one gulp.

"Thanks...needed that," he mumbled and slouched in his chair. "You going to untie me?"

She tilted her head to one side and regarded him with a serious expression, eye looking him up and down, noting his body language and the set of his chin. "Not until you promise not to try to kill me."

"Now why would I kill my own sister?" Marcas scoffed and looked away.

"Because she thought it best to destroy your ship," Rhona replied. "I'm not daft, Marcas. I can tell when you're murderous."

Marcas sat there for a few minutes without saying anything. Rhona was happy to let him think. He would eventually understand that she did what had to be done and be grateful for her initiative. She'd wanted to stick around to see if all the blood from Dawkins's intimate acquaintance with the *Ebon Drake*'s hull and the activity of the burning ship would call up a beast from the Deep, but she'd been much more eager to find her brother. It was fortuitous, all of it. She didn't want to imagine what might have happened to Marcas if she hadn't been able to rescue him from that tiny island. He would have wasted away from hunger, and she never would have known!

"What are you going to do with my friend?" Marcas asked, breaking the silence.

"What would you like me to do with him?"

"I don't want him harmed or killed. And he's to stay with me in your guest cabin."

Rhona nodded. "If he's truly your friend, as you say, and not a courtier of the Crakesydian king's that you intend to ransom, then I've no problems with that request."

"You have my word that he's not a courtier, that I don't intend to ransom him, and that he's my friend," Marcas said.

A hard gaze into Marcas's eyes filled her with shock. He was telling the truth!

"Either Morris is keeping something from me or you are, brother dear," she said, eye narrowed at him. "Morris doesn't have any reason to keep things from me. He's afraid of the consequences."

"He's also a jealous ninny," Marcas drawled.

Rhona refilled the glass with rum and turned to smirk at her brother. "Do tell!"

"That simpering little maggot was always flirting with me and trying to get me to bed him."

"And why didn't you?" Rhona let him have another sip of rum, but took the glass away to let him speak.

Marcas shrugged. "Trying not to mix business with pleasure."

"According to Morris that's exactly what pushed the men to mutiny. They were all convinced you were doing delicious things to your very own prisoner behind closed doors. In fact, Morris insists you've fallen in love with Mr. Smith, which would explain your promoting him from prisoner to a guest on your ship." Rhona took a small taste of the rum herself then, but made sure to watch her brother's face carefully. She was well aware that she had more information than he expected her to have. It was still bothering her, however, that all of her information wasn't adding up in a logical way.

"Love? Don't be ridiculous," Marcas rolled his eyes and stared at his sister with a bored expression. "As I said, we're friends."

"So it was all a simple change of heart? Marcas, you're getting soft. I'm disappointed in you! The ransom idea was brilliant, one of the best you've had…well ever. And you gave it up for *friendship*?"

The look on his face was all she needed to see to know he was the one keeping secrets. He visibly balked at what she said, but didn't seem to want to refute it either. She couldn't imagine what the real reason behind his changing his mind about the ransom could be. There wouldn't be any reason for him to hide any sexual conquests from her. In fact, he usually bragged about whomever he'd slept with.

"I promise not to kill you if you untie me," Marcas said after another awkward silence.

CHAPTER 12

"How did you end up here?" Gavin asked Morris after he'd been released from a cell in the *Crimson Wake*'s brig. The ship was much larger than the *Ebon Drake*, and the cells were made out of metal bars instead of wooden walls.

"The queen found us an' I was the only one clever enough to join up with her crew." The cabin boy's voice was as smug as his smile.

"So you're a mutineer twice over," Gavin said blandly. He wasn't any more impressed with the young scamp now than he had been when they'd first met on Marcas's ship.

"You're real lucky for a redhead. Lucky I'm under her majesty's orders not to knock your teeth in," Morris said and then spat on the stairs in disgust as they walked up.

"Still pining after Captain Drake then?" Gavin was unsurprised, even given the mutiny. It was a cheap shot to take at the boy, but he made an effort to crush any vindictive feelings that might have powered his jibe. What he'd done with Marcas while they were on the island was of no consequence now. With the island far behind them, he was unsure how he felt about the pirate. There was more hope of returning home, which meant he would eventually have to tell his father what he knew about his captors. He supposed he could lie to his father and blame the entire kidnapping plot on the Crimson Queen, but he didn't want to lie to his father any more than he wanted to be responsible for the hanging of Marcas's sister.

Gavin was so wrapped up in his own thoughts that he didn't notice Morris hadn't bothered to answer his question.

"Did you know that the Crimson Queen and Captain Drake were siblings?" he asked as they ascended the final flight of stairs to the main deck of the ship.

"Yeah. Her majesty told me the first day I was her cabin boy," Morris said. "They look like brother and sister so it's not surprising. Oh and I always heard Angus Drake had a daughter what tried to save his life in his final duel."

"But she lost her eye, and he lost his life..." Gavin recalled the story quite clearly now that Morris mentioned it. He never would have thought to connect the most well-known female pirate of the day with Angus Drake's swashbuckling daughter.

"Tha's right. She's got a nice eye patch though; did you see? It's all encrusted with gems. I think it makes the queen look even more like royalty."

Before Gavin could reply, they'd crossed the deck and stood at the ornately carved and painted doors to the captain's cabin. Morris knocked three times and then announced who he was and his business. The door swung inward to reveal a tired-looking Marcas and a lavish cabin interior.

"Gavin, come in," Marcas said, gesturing to the cabin with the glass of what could only be rum in his hand. He scowled at Morris. "Maggot, fetch my coat."

Gavin hesitated to enter the cabin, not wanting to be in

the middle of any altercation. He didn't like the dark look in Marcas's eyes.

"I don't take orders from you no more," Morris said and glared right back at his former captain.

"You'll do as my brother says while he's on my ship, Morris." The Crimson Queen's stern voice came from inside the cabin.

Morris hurried off without further protest as Gavin gave Marcas a weak smile and joined him before the queen.

"You're sure I can't run him through?" Marcas asked his sister once he'd closed the door again. He resumed his seat in the comfortable upholstered chair and took a swig of his rum.

"I need him, Marcas," Rhona replied. She gestured for Gavin to take a seat in the matching chair beside Marcas.

Gavin looked more than a little uneasy. It wasn't a good situation for him, and depending on how many prodding questions Rhona asked him, it could get worse. Marcas wasn't in a good situation either. He wanted to drink as much rum as his sister would give him and pass out. Then, at least for a time, he wouldn't have to deal with the fact that his ship was gone forever. His father's own glory, a birthday gift stolen from an Anthean princess. The only true home he'd ever known. There was more sentimental value attached to that outdated ship than anything else. She was irreplaceable, and sentimental value aside, where was he going to get a new ship? And who would be foolish enough to sign up to be part of his crew now? As soon as the *Crimson Wake* made port, he was sure Morris and plenty of Rhona's other crew members would tell the story of his remarkably bad luck to anyone who would listen.

"Let me know when you're tired of his fumbling. I'll cut his mutinous head off." Marcas couldn't mask the snarl that had taken up residence on his face. The little bastard would get what was coming to him, sure enough. It was Marcas's pity on the boy that had allowed him to be a sailor in the first place. Morris had reminded him of himself when he was young, but apparently Marcas hadn't taught him anything outside self-preservation. He had trouble understanding how his sense of loyalty had failed to rub off on the maggot.

"Of course, Marcas," Rhona said with a giggle. She handed Gavin a glass of rum and poured another for herself. "Now, Gavin, have we met before?"

Marcas smirked. His sister would try anything and everything to figure out Gavin's place in all this, but she would fail. It was impossible for them to have met before.

Gavin held on to his glass with both hands for a moment, studying Rhona before glancing at Marcas.

"I don't think so...Your Highness," Gavin said. At least he knew how to play the game. That, in and of itself, would buy him more time if Rhona decided to renege on her deal to leave Gavin alone.

Rhona set her glass of rum down on a small table, clasped both of her bejewelled hands beneath her chin, and stared at Gavin. "Darling you're terribly familiar, and redheads are so uncommon out in the world. You're not from New Auchen, are you? If you are, I'm terribly sorry about the state we left the town in, but it was a necessary bit of pirating, you understand."

Gavin shook his head. "No, Your Highness, I'm not from New Auchen."

He glanced at Marcas again, but it wasn't as if Marcas could give him the right answers with his sister sitting there in front of them. She was so unpredictable that he didn't know the right answers himself.

"Marcas assures me you're not a courtier, but your clothing looks expensive, and well tailored. High fashion in Crakesyde, if I'm not mistaken, and I hardly ever am," Rhona carried on. She got up and took a few steps closer to Gavin, circling him like a predator preparing to pounce.

"You're not mistaken about my clothes," Gavin said grudgingly, watching Rhona as she walked beside him. He looked as if he wished she'd mentioned anything else about his appearance besides his outfit.

Suddenly Rhona bent over and grabbed Gavin by the chin, forcing him to face forward again so she could look at him in profile. He didn't struggle, but he did try to lean away when she kissed him on the cheek. She straightened up, clapped her hands excitedly, and then reached into a pouch on her belt and pulled out a gold coin.

"A ha!" she shouted, her voice increasing in pitch to a near screech. She tossed the coin to Marcas, who caught it and looked down at it.

"Thanks, I'm broke," Marcas said and made to pocket the coin, but Rhona waggled a finger at him.

"Look at it!" she commanded, her voice still giddy. "I knew I recognised that nose! It's my favourite nose in the world. And your weak chin, Gavin, it's a dead giveaway when the rest of you is taken into consideration."

Sure enough, to Marcas's horror, the profile of a youthful King Malcolm on every Crakesydian gold coin was practically the same as Gavin's. Or vice versa, considering the king was his father. He felt stupid then because he'd never really paid attention to what the king looked like.

"Marcas, it's too bad I got all the brains, or else you would've realised a long time ago that you're friends with Crakesydian royalty," Rhona said and laughed. She turned her attention back to a terrified Gavin. "Prince Gavin! It's no wonder you became fast friends with Marcas, since he's royalty as well."

"Rhona...I wish you'd quit that," Marcas muttered into his glass of rum. It was fine for her to have crowned herself the Pirate Queen, but he didn't want any part of that particular mad notion of hers.

"Marcas! How many times do I have to tell you? There's nothing to be ashamed of about your superior status! Daddy was king of the pirates, and I've inherited that throne. Which makes you a prince. It's all very simple!" Rhona said, snatching the gold coin back from her brother.

"*You* were his princess, Rhona. I was the lost cause. Remember?" Marcas said through clenched teeth. He didn't want to bring up old family drama in front of Gavin, but being around his sister always put him on the defensive. It was one of the main reasons he'd taken to avoiding her in the first place.

"Daddy loved us both just the same," Rhona said, looking near tears. She sighed and shook her head. "Gavin, I'm sorry my brother's being so sour. He's had a lot of bad news today, and he's still broken up over Daddy's death even after all these years."

"It's quite all right, Your Highness," Gavin said, though he looked as if he wanted to get as far away from her as possible instead of carrying on a semi-polite conversation.

"I, on the other hand, have had an excellent day." Rhona fanned her hand over her heart, as if to still any fluttering. "I've found my brother, safe and sound, and my future husband all in one day!"

Gavin and Marcas turned to look at one another in shared confusion.

"Please tell me you're going to marry...Morris," Marcas said and tried to force a laugh.

Rhona's giggling was less than encouraging.

"Don't be silly, Marcas! I'm going to marry Prince Gavin here, of course. We'll combine our kingdoms, Crakesyde and the sea, and together we'll rule at least three quarters of the world! Doesn't that sound delightful, Gavin dear?" She grinned at Gavin and Marcas in turn, delighted with her grandiose scheme.

"But… I… My father…" Gavin stammered, unable to get a complete thought out through his shock.

"We'll travel the globe as queen and king of the pirates until your father passes on, then I'll—"

"Rhona you can't marry him," Marcas said, cutting her off mid-sentence. He stood up and prepared for her wrath. It was nothing he couldn't handle. A lot of screaming in his face and threats, but she would never do more than slap him around.

"And why not? It's my right as queen to expand my territories through marriage," she said sternly. He could sense her ire rising. She never could take no for an answer.

"I don't think the current king of Crakesyde would agree to that sort of political arrangement," Marcas said.

"I'm sure he would if he wants to ensure his heir's continued safety," she countered with a sweet smile.

"What about our deal?" It was Marcas's turn to get angry.

She walked over to him and touched his cheek. "Marcas, darling, I know the real reason behind that deal of yours. There's no use lying to me about it because I can see it in the way you look at him," she said. It was as if she'd forgotten Gavin was even there. "You know very well that marriage is all about property rights. If you two want to carry on being lovers, I'd be perfectly happy for you both, so long as there are legally binding documents saying my property is combined with his."

Marcas grabbed his sister's hand and pulled it slowly away from his face. She didn't flinch. "I told you we're *friends*.

And I care about what few friends I have. That was the reason for my deal."

A knock at the door interrupted any further conversation. Rhona opened the door wide to let a few of her crew bring in platters of food and tableware, plus Marcas's coat. Marcas was doubly glad for the intrusion. He was hungry and tired of his sister ruining what progress he'd made with Gavin. The prince wouldn't be anything but annoyed at the idea of them being lovers or the word love being involved in their relationship at all. It had been hard enough to get him to agree they were friends.

As they sat down and began to eat without any ceremony, Marcas wondered why he was still going through with his stupid idea to woo Gavin. It had been a bit of a distraction at first, something to while away a lot of empty travelling time as they searched for a merchant ship to plunder. Once they got to the island, it had been further distraction from the harsh realities he'd been trying not to face. Now, the mutiny seemed nothing compared with the true loss of his ship. Before, there had been some hope he would recover the *Ebon Drake*, manage to find a more loyal crew and better luck, while he was at it. Now there was nothing to do but loaf off his sister's hospitality until he just couldn't stand it anymore. Which meant there was no more reason for him to seduce Gavin, except out of cruelty.

What he needed to focus on now was helping Gavin get safely home again.

"I don't know what this is, but it's the most delicious thing I've ever tasted," Gavin said. His happiness over having real food again must have made his fears melt away. "Your cook is amazing, Your Highness."

Marcas nodded his agreement, but he didn't stop stuffing his face long enough to talk.

CHAPTER 13

GRATEFUL DIDN'T EVEN BEGIN TO COVER HOW GAVIN FELT when Marcas excused them from the Crimson Queen's cabin after dinner. If he paused to think about what a predicament he was in, he was sure he'd stop functioning all together. There was too much going on, and he didn't have control over any of it. It was maddening to be told by some barmy pirate he was going to marry her. And her implications about his and Marcas's relationship were just as bad.

"The way her mind works... It's completely absurd! What does she do, stare at money all day?" Gavin said once they were in the privacy of the guest cabin and Marcas had locked them in.

"She's the greediest pirate I know," Marcas said and kicked his boots off near the door. He opened up the lone trunk in the room and was rewarded with a full bottle of rum.

Gavin was a bit put off by Marcas's seeming lack of concern for his new situation. Of course the woman who'd put him in this situation was the pirate's own sister. He took in the furnishings of the modest little cabin. It was larger than the one he'd been in on board the *Ebon Drake*, but smaller than Marcas's cabin had been. He was surprised, yet somewhat pleased, to see that instead of a hammock, a bed with a high side on it dominated the room. There was also the chest Marcas had rummaged through, a small desk with a single wooden chair tucked beneath it, and a single lantern hung from the ceiling.

"What sort of deal did you make with your sister?" Gavin asked. He hated how tired his voice sounded, but their day had been a long one, and he was ready to sleep. The bed looked so inviting with its pillows and red quilted blanket. He took his shoes off and set them near Marcas's boots.

"That you're not to be harmed, and you stay with me in my cabin," he replied and took a swig of rum.

"Thank you," Gavin said and smiled weakly. No matter his original intentions, things had come to a point where one day he would have to repay Marcas for his kindness. He hoped that would include saving him from a trip to the gallows.

"Get some rest. We'll need clear heads if we're going to come up with a way to get you home again before my sister decides she doesn't need your father's consent before marrying you," Marcas said. He corked the rum after one more sip and tucked the bottle back in the trunk.

Gavin nodded and crawled onto the bed, making sure to leave as much room as possible for Marcas. The bed didn't look like it was meant for more than one person, but Gavin knew they'd be at least ten times more comfortable sandwiched together on a mattress than on some leaves and sand. He heard Marcas extinguish the candle in the lantern and then felt him lie down beside him. Gavin rolled onto his side to give the other man more room if he wanted to sleep on his back.

Marcas's hand fumbled over Gavin's shoulder in the dark,

finding his neck, chin, and lips. Before Gavin could ask what he was doing, the pirate had closed what little gap there was between them and kissed him gently. It was a strange kiss, unlike any of the other ones they'd shared, and Gavin found himself reaching out to touch Marcas without thought. He wanted to reassure both Marcas and himself that they were safe for the moment. Safe and together, adrift in a sea of madness. He found Marcas's chest first, trailing his hand over his shirt until his arm draped over the other man's torso.

Marcas pulled away and shifted onto his other side before Gavin had a chance to get comfortable.

"I don't mind," Gavin said quietly and scooted over until he pressed comfortably against Marcas's back, his arm still draped over the other man's side.

"Let's try just being friends now that it's much more likely you'll end up having to explain my kidnapping you to your father," Marcas said.

Gavin started to think Marcas was being overly serious, but the pirate laughed a little after he spoke. He wasn't sure how to reply to that. It had been on his mind as well; the future of their friendship looked increasingly grim, but why would that make Marcas suddenly decide they needed to distance themselves from one another? Hadn't that been Gavin's idea in the first place? Hadn't Marcas called the idea ridiculous and made the point that they could be friends regardless of any attraction they felt? But that had been while they thought they were stuck on the island permanently. Everything had changed, yet again, now that they'd been rescued.

"Marcas?"

"Hm?"

"There was something your sister said…about how you'd

had a lot of bad news?" Gavin hadn't wanted to ask while they were still in the queen's presence. She made him feel insignificant, the same way his father did. As if he was a mere pawn and not a person. If he had disliked her by reputation alone, he loathed the woman in a very personal manner now.

There was silence in the cabin. Gavin thought Marcas had fallen asleep.

"She burned my ship with the crew inside," Marcas ground out. Gavin could tell it took a lot of strength for him to even speak the words, and he couldn't begin to fathom what was going through Marcas's mind. That ship was his life. *Had been* his life.

"So you're trapped here the same as I am," Gavin whispered.

"Seems like our kind of luck," Marcas whispered back.

THE EARLY MORNING sun shone through the cabin's little window, even though thin curtains had been drawn across it. Marcas lay there, staring at the ceiling, and tried not to think about anything. He'd slept hard for most of the night, but kept having strange dreams that woke him once the first hints of dawn's light brightened the cabin. The worst of the dreams had been of his sister making him her cabin boy again, like she had for the brief time she'd been the captain of the *Ebon Drake*. In that same dream, he'd been the one to marry Rhona to Gavin, and then his mutinous crew, every one of them still ablaze, crashed the wedding and set the *Crimson Wake* to follow his ship's fate.

He kept coming up blank whenever he tried to think of a way to get Gavin and himself off his sister's ship. He could promise he'd take Gavin back to Crakesyde with the sole purpose of garnering King Malcolm's consent for his son to marry her. Yet he assumed Rhona had her own ideas of how to persuade the king, and they likely involved direct attacks on navy vessels. She was too fond of making a show of overpowering pirate hunters and navy ships, and it would be a great way for her to get the king's attention.

A part of him wondered if that shouldn't have been his course of action in the first place, but he knew the *Ebon Drake* wasn't hearty enough to square off against a royal navy ship.

Or hadn't been, as it were.

He sighed and closed his eyes again. Maybe if he pretended to fall back to sleep long enough he actually would.

"All right?" Gavin said, his voice groggy from sleep. He shifted to face Marcas again instead of the wall.

"As much as I can be," Marcas said. "Would be much better if I could think of a decent plan to get us off this bloody ship."

"We could jump ship at the next port and not come back," Gavin suggested with a shrug and then yawned. He buried his face in the bit of pillow by Marcas's shoulder and mumbled into it. "Daft idea, I know. Who knows when that'll happen."

"No... No, that's brilliant. Simple, means less chance to fail. Especially if we're quick about setting sail on some other ship," Marcas said. He caught himself smiling and didn't even care that he hadn't thought of it first.

"But we've got two pistols, a cutlass, and some clothes between the two of us. Can't book passage on a ship with that," Gavin said, tilting his face towards Marcas again.

"You're the prince of Crakesyde, Gavin. I'll pretend to be your manservant if that's what it takes, but a prince should be able to get a free ride."

"That's silly. You *didn't* sleep well, did you?" Gavin said with a humoured little grin. "I don't think anyone besides your sister would believe I'm who I am while I look like this."

"Like what? Like you need to shave?" Marcas smirked.

"Not any more than you do," Gavin shot back. He reached over to feel the thick black stubble on Marcas's cheek for emphasis.

"At least I know how to shave with a knife."

"I'm used to having soap," Gavin said defensively. "Besides, I couldn't grow a decent beard if I wanted to. Which my sister finds hilarious. I think I'd look awful with loads of facial hair anyway."

Marcas shrugged. "Rhona goes a bit overboard with cleanliness. She's got a washroom on one of the lower decks for officers and guests. So we can return to being our usual handsome selves today."

Gavin laughed. "Just remember you can't kill Morris if he starts making passes at you again."

SEVERAL DAYS PASSED FAIRLY UNEVENTFULLY. Rhona had become so caught up in planning her own wedding that she'd left Gavin and Marcas to themselves outside of meal times. Table conversations were strained, but at least she'd made mention of the next port they were going to visit. Any actual details on how she planned to communicate with King Malcolm she kept to herself, and Gavin wasn't about to ask her outright just in case she asked him for any private details about his family.

Gavin and Marcas were awakened in the middle of the night by the distinct sound of cannons being fired and the ship rocking sharply. Gavin bolted upright in bed and tried to wait for his eyes to adjust to the dark. Faint moonlight shone in through the curtain, but it wasn't helping. Another burst of cannon fire sounded outside.

"What's going on? Are we being attacked?"

"Put your shoes on. Quick!" Marcas said, taking on his commanding captain's tone. He jumped out of bed, fumbled to put on his boots and find his weapons and coat, and then unlocked the door and took a few steps onto the deck.

Gavin followed suit, trying to be as quick as possible. He hoped they were the ones doing the attacking, unless of course, it was a navy ship. In that case, he wasn't even sure who he'd prefer to come out the victor.

Marcas shoved one of his pistols into Gavin's hand. He wished someone would give him a rapier, something he could actually use to defend himself.

"Looks like we're taking on a merchantman," Marcas said loudly, making sure Gavin could hear him over all the activity on board.

The crew ran around, following all manner of orders shouted out by their captain that Gavin could barely understand. Some of the terms were nautical in nature, but the queen seemed to have taken on a lowlier accent than the one she usually spoke with. He reminded himself to ask Marcas later, when they knew they were relatively safe again, how it was that he and his sister were so well spoken.

"Are they firing back?" Gavin asked, but his question was drowned out by another round of cannon fire. He was mesmerised by the sight of cannon balls shooting over to the other ship in a burst of smoke and sparks.

"Stay here. I've got to help Rhona," Marcas said and dashed off across the deck.

Gavin had no qualms about staying put and near as he was to the cabin door, he could duck back inside if he felt so inclined. Still, he had to wonder why they were using cannons on a merchant ship. If the queen wanted to secure the merchantman's plunder, she'd have to keep the ship afloat. Of course, the woman was deranged, so there was no telling what she was thinking. Logic was not her strong suit.

CHAPTER 14

"Sending over a boarding party, or are you going to turn it to kindling?" Marcas asked Rhona.

"It's like old times again! Brother and sister, taking what we can and having no pity for fools who try to stop us!" Rhona said with a laugh and drew her sword. "Feel free to join us, of course!"

"I will," Marcas said. He cocked his pistol, ready for the boarding to begin at any moment. They'd already drawn alongside the merchantman and fired a few volleys from the great guns. The merchant ship had retaliated once with her own cannons, but didn't seem to have done much damage.

"Grenadiers, ready…and fire!" Rhona called out.

A deluge of lit grenades launched at the deck of the other ship. Small explosions sent what was left of their crew scattering and screaming in pain. The resulting smoke would also help their eminent boarding of the merchant ship. Rhona called for the men by the rails to toss their grappling irons. Then it was only a matter of time until the two ships were lashed together with rope. The grenadiers fired another volley of grenades before the boarding party charged onto the other ship, pistols firing and cutlasses drawn. Marcas waited until some of the other men had run across the planks now connecting the two ships before boarding himself. It was never a good idea to be first to board unless you were sure the crew had retreated to closed quarters, and it was obvious before the second set of grenades covered the merchant deck with smoke that a good portion of the merchant crew were waiting to defend their ship.

To reassure himself, he patted the vest pocket concealing an envelope bearing precious cargo: the ransom letter Gavin had penned so long ago. Once across the breach, Marcas had his own mission, aside from staying alive.

He fired his pistol almost immediately, catching a man in the neck. Quickly, he holstered the gun and drew his cutlass. Another man sought to block his path, but Marcas ran him through and shoved him aside before the sailor could pretend he knew what he was doing with a sword. Winding his way between private wars being waged all across the deck, he found the captain's cabin. He snatched the envelope out of his pocket and shoved it between the doors. A pistol shot sailed past his head and shattered the right door's window. He whipped around.

Sword at the ready, he rushed on the man he guessed had fired at him. This one seemed to know how to fight, and Marcas found himself on the defensive more than he liked. Just as he regained the upper hand and moved the sailor back with each offensive slash, an errant pistol shot caught the sailor in the leg. The sailor hopped back on one foot, howling in pain. Marcas disarmed him and shoved him towards the railing of the ship. Not caring if the sailor went overboard, he headed back across the main deck towards the *Crimson Wake*. The smoke had cleared, making it plain the boarding party outnumbered the crew of the merchant ship. Rhona's pirates had nearly brought the fighting to a standstill with their sheer numbers, so it was easy for Marcas to cross back over to his sister's ship.

"That went well," he said to Rhona as he met her again.

She took to checking him over for injuries. Once satisfied that he seemed whole, she grinned and nodded. "Now to find the captain and hope, for his sake, that he isn't cheeky."

She giggled and hurried across to the other ship. Arreid was on her tail, watchful as ever. At least Marcas didn't have to worry about his sister's well-being with him around.

Since the rest of the action was up to the Crimson Queen and her crew, Marcas decided to play the passenger card and headed back to his cabin. When he didn't immediately spot Gavin where he'd left him, he became nervous. What if he'd been caught up in the boarding party somehow? But he found the door to the cabin locked and heaved a sigh of relief.

"All right in there?" he asked the door after knocking on it. He heard the key turn in the lock, and then the door opened a fraction. Once Gavin saw it was indeed Marcas, he was allowed in.

"I don't know how you do this," Gavin said and sat down on the end of the bed.

Marcas locked the door and set the key on the desk next to his second pistol, which he picked up and secured to its proper place over his chest. He took a seat on the wooden chair and shrugged.

"Better than being a blacksmith," Marcas said. "Not nearly as safe, but generally pays more to make up for it."

"What's blacksmithing have to do with anything?" Gavin turned sideways on the end of the bed to better see Marcas.

"That's what I was supposed to do." Marcas slouched down in his chair. He contemplated getting out the rum, but he wanted to be sure he wouldn't be needed in some emergency situation before he drank in earnest. The light from the lantern showed Gavin's confused expression. "It's a well-kept secret that me and Rhona were adopted by Angus Drake. He'd lost his own wife and kids to a hurricane a few years before he raided our colony. Our parents died in a fire, so far as we know, and Rhona thought it'd be a great idea to hide out on the *Ebon Drake* and take our revenge on Deadeye Angus ourselves."

"Marcas…why are you telling me this if it's a secret?"

"Rhona's the only one who cares. Everyone else who knew is dead now, so why not share the truth with my friend?" His only friend. Rhona… She'd never willingly hurt him in any meaningful sense of the word, but that didn't make a friendship. She was too far gone.

"How old were you?"

"Eight, I think? Rhona was around ten. Anyway, our revenge plot was foiled when the crew found us shortly after setting sail. Luckily old Angus was reminded of his own children and claimed us as his own. I think the shift was too hard for Rhona to handle, and that's what addled her brains. She really believes Angus Drake is our father. She punched me in the face once for suggesting otherwise." Marcas laughed, remembering that particular fat lip very well.

"That's an amazing story," Gavin said, awed.

"I know. Which is why I need to make sure it doesn't die with me and my sister." Marcas smirked. Sometimes he felt like he outdid himself. When that ransom letter found its way back to Crakesyde, the royal navy would be after them. Then it would only be a matter of time before Gavin was on his way home again.

"Please tell me you're not planning on dying any time soon," Gavin said, suddenly terse.

Hearing calm voices outside, Marcas took off his weapons, set them on top of the trunk, and then crossed over to sit on the bed next to Gavin.

"In my line of work there's always a chance I'll be dead before I'm ready, but I never plan on it," he said. Then he kicked his boots off and stretched out on the bed. From the general lack of pistol and cannon fire, Marcas assumed all was going well with the looting of the merchant ship. That meant he was free to relax.

A few moments later, Gavin lay down beside him so they were shoulder to shoulder. The lull in conversation allowed Marcas to drift off to a light sleep.

"I wonder what sort of cargo they're carrying." Gavin's words brought Marcas back to the waking world.

"Now you sound like a pirate." Marcas chuckled and shifted on his side of the bed until he'd turned towards Gavin and draped an arm across Gavin's narrow chest.

Gavin ran his hand over Marcas's arm affectionately, fingers splaying in lazy, abstract patterns. "I don't think I'd make a very good pirate. I'm not interested in risking my life any more than I have to, and I need to be concerned with how piracy affects the economy and the working man."

"Sounds dull."

"I doubt my life will be dull so long as you're in it."

"You make it sound like a bad thing." Marcas forced one of his eyes open and tried to make out whether or not Gavin was smiling. He wasn't, but he hadn't put on his serious face either. He looked more concerned than anything, which Marcas found odd but endearing.

"I'm not sure," Gavin said quietly. He bit his lip and turned to face Marcas. In the dim lighting, he seemed to be searching Marcas's face for some sort of hint of how to feel. "I didn't like watching you run over to that other ship with all the pistol shots going off and fighting going on."

"I'm all right. Done it plenty of times before. I know what I'm doing," Marcas said with a smirk. Gavin's genuine concern for his well-being was amusing.

"For some reason that's not reassuring," Gavin said wryly.

"You really got scared for me, didn't you?"

"Well, yes. You're the only friend I have on this ship. If you were killed, I'd never have a chance of getting off this ship without ending up married to your sister." Gavin sighed and closed his eyes.

But Marcas wasn't fooled by any attempts on Gavin's part to pretend he was trying to fall asleep. He leaned over and kissed Gavin on the corner of his mouth.

"What was that for?" Gavin mumbled and kept his eyes closed.

"Trying to reassure you is all," Marcas whispered in his ear and kissed him again, this time on the side of his neck. "Is it working?"

"Your sister and most of her crew are committing acts of piracy just outside our door, and all you can think about is seducing me?" Gavin laughed, though it almost sounded like one of his drunken giggles.

"Have you been drinking?" Marcas asked, surprised.

"Not much," Gavin shrugged.

"I swear you're slowly turning into a pirate. First wondering about what kind of plunder's on the merchantman, and now you've got a taste for rum," Marcas said and laughed against Gavin's shoulder. "Next you'll be the newest member of the *Wake*'s boarding party!"

"You just want me to be a pirate," Gavin said, smirking up at the ceiling.

"Really?" Marcas laughed again. "Why's that?"

"So we can remain friends," Gavin said, but the way he emphasised "friends," drawing the word out deliberately, made Marcas think he meant something else entirely.

"You think I only want you around so I can seduce you?" Marcas said, borrowing Gavin's own phrasing. For some reason the conversation had lost its humour. He wasn't sure why he was offended by Gavin's implications, considering at one time such implications would have been correct, but he wasn't worried about figuring out his own reasoning.

"It's crossed my mind," Gavin said and turned away from Marcas. The jovial mood had been ruined for him as well.

Marcas opened his mouth to say he wanted Gavin around for more than the potential of sex, but the words died on his lips. Nothing he could think of to say was free of innuendo. Gavin was far from right, of course. Marcas liked him, wanted to carry on with their strange friendship as long as he possibly could, and sure he wouldn't mind if one thing led to another now and again. He supposed a lot of it had to do with his being able to trust Gavin.

"You're wrong," Marcas said.

"I know," Gavin said quietly.

"Well then. Maybe it's you who really wants me to stick around for a little seduction," Marcas said, shaking his head at his own accusation. He knew Gavin was telling the truth about why he was concerned for Marcas's safety.

"Partly," Gavin said, his voice still barely above a whisper. Marcas wasn't even sure he'd heard him right at first and scooted closer to him again.

"I am rather charming," Marcas said just as softly.

"Only when you're not trying to be," Gavin said and laughed lightly. He sounded relieved the conversation wasn't so serious anymore.

"If this is your seduction technique, it's not a very good one," Marcas said. He kissed Gavin's shoulder and ran his hand down his arm.

"Seems to be working fine if you ask me," Gavin said.

"I sort of miss the island," Marcas admitted. Now that he knew his ship was gone and he would likely hang before the year was out, the idea of being stuck back on that island seemed like a dream. On the island, they'd been somewhat carefree once they'd accepted the idea they might never leave. Now their problems could only weigh them down again, and neither one of them seemed to set them aside for very long, even in the privacy of their own cabin.

"So do I." Gavin moved enough to see Marcas over his shoulder. "Which is ironic, considering I would have done anything to get away from there."

"Anything but marry the Crimson Queen," Marcas said and laughed again.

"Don't remind me, please," Gavin said with a heavy sigh. He rolled his eyes. "I'm just waiting for her to start talking about producing heirs."

"I'll remind her bastards don't count," Marcas said. He wasn't about to let his sister lay her hands on Gavin in that way. In fact, he startled himself with his suddenly possessive thoughts. He didn't want to think about the possibility of *anyone* besides himself being intimate with Gavin. The possessive feeling was so strong that he had to wonder where his reason had gone. Maybe he was feeling desperate to hold on to any hope he could keep Gavin in his life now that he had nothing else left to look forward to. But he mentally berated himself for being so fatalistic. He wasn't swinging from the gallows yet. There was time enough left for them to try to escape the *Crimson Wake*.

"Thank you," Gavin said sleepily. He studied Marcas's face in the low lantern light for a moment, brows furrowed. "You look vexed."

Marcas kissed Gavin's cheek lightly. "I was just thinking you were right about your seduction technique working."

"That's funny, because I was joking about having one at all," Gavin said and grinned. He turned and kissed Marcas properly, reaching up one hand to hold his bristly cheek.

"Maybe seduction's not the right word for it then," Marcas mumbled against Gavin's lips before kissing Gavin again. This time he let his lips linger, being sure to savour the moment.

"I don't understand," Gavin said, pulling back. He looked at Marcas with his brows furrowed and waited for an explanation.

Marcas didn't have one. He shrugged one shoulder. "I'm not sure I understand myself."

"Marcas, are you trying to say you're in love with me?" Gavin asked, his tone flat with disbelief.

"I think I might be," he replied, quirking one brow thoughtfully. It was the only thing that made any semblance of sense given his ridiculous thoughts.

Gavin stared at him, giving Marcas time to mull the idea over a little more as he studied Gavin's face. He hated to think his mutinous cabin boy and his sister had noticed before he'd even had a chance to realise it for himself. Of course, there was the general irony regarding his failed attempts to woo Gavin. Everything he'd tried to do lately backfired. Love, at least, couldn't be all bad.

"You're sure you don't just want to have sex with me?" Gavin finally said. He sounded like he'd been mentally running through any reason he could find for Marcas to be wrong.

"Yes." Marcas grinned, amused, and hooked his arm fully around Gavin. "I keep having crazy ideas about how to keep you safe, how to get you back to your family, and how I'd rather be hanged than not have you in my life. So you can see my dilemma."

The look in Gavin's eyes was one of pure fear. At first Marcas was confused by how tense his body had become, but then he remembered Gavin's old-fashioned views about romantic love's existence.

"You're serious," Gavin whispered. He shook his head. "That's… No, you have to be mistaken."

"I could be. I've never been in love before, I don't think. Of course I know what lust feels like, and it doesn't usually involve my wanting to stick around after the sex."

"We haven't exactly had actual sex yet," Gavin said quickly. Too quickly. Even in the bad lighting, Marcas could see his cheeks had darkened in a flush. "I mean…not that it's inevitable. Just that it could happen and it hasn't."

"You're the king of mixed signals," Marcas said and kissed him again. He wasn't surprised Gavin made no real effort to return the sentiment.

Marcas slid to the end of the bed, got up, and doused the lantern's candle. When he returned to bed, he kept to his own side of the mattress. He didn't want to come off as pushy just then, and he was tired, after all.

"What if I'm not in love with you?" Gavin sounded unsure of himself.

"Then you'll have one less thing to worry about."

CHAPTER 15

AFTER THE SUCCESSFUL PLUNDERING OF THE MERCHANTMAN'S valuables and rum, it only took two more days for the *Crimson Wake* to make berth at Morbryde. Gavin would have been relieved to finally be able to set foot on land again, but he'd been given strict orders from his self-proclaimed fiancée to stay on board the ship. She had repairs to arrange and money to spend, or so she'd said.

Gavin was unhappy with himself for being so caught up in trying to figure out his feelings for Marcas that he'd failed to think once on how they were going to get off the ship unseen. Now his escape plan seemed more ridiculous than when he'd proposed it.

"Do you think she'd keelhaul me if she caught me leaving the ship?" he asked Marcas once they were both back in their cabin after breakfast with her highness.

"Not a chance," Marcas said, scoffing at the idea. He gave Gavin a serious look then. "But she would introduce you to her cat o' nine tails without blinking."

Gavin frowned. He wasn't interested in being whipped until he was bloody. There was no doubt in his mind: the queen would not hold back. Just because she wanted to marry him wouldn't have any bearing on how viciously she'd punish him for a slight. That meant they'd have to be especially sneaky. "How are we going to get off the ship together without being seen?"

"What we need is a distraction," Marcas said. "If we could make sure what crew's left on board is busy, then we could sneak away."

"Did your sister give you any money?" Gavin knew Marcas had asked to borrow some of her gold to hold him over until he'd managed to begin again with a new ship and crew of his own.

"Some, but not enough to pay for 'no questions asked' on a ship headed that far east," Marcas said with a shrug. "We might have to earn our passage if they don't believe you're you."

"You mean…help sail the ship?" Gavin swallowed hard. He'd seen a crew in action of course, on two different ships no less, but that did little more than make him realise he wasn't cut out to be a sailor.

"That sort of thing, yes. Don't look surprised! It's not so hard." Marcas nodded and smiled at Gavin. It was likely supposed to be reassuring, but made Gavin more certain he'd make a fool of himself and get hurt if that were the case.

"You've been doing it your whole life, Marcas; of course it's easy for you."

The pirate shrugged again and smirked. "We can argue later. I've just had a better idea than a distraction. Let's wander around below decks and see if we can't climb through a gun port."

Gavin gladly let Marcas lead the way. He tried to stay as quiet as possible, knowing some of the crew had stayed behind to sleep or keep watch. They passed a single snoring man with a bottle of rum in hand, much to Gavin's relief. He was sure no one would question Marcas, but that didn't mean they wouldn't report whatever they'd seen to the queen, no matter how benign.

Marcas wasted no time. He lifted a hatch and stuck his head out of a gun port. Ducking back in, he raised an eyebrow at him.

"Do you know how to swim?"

"Yes, of course, but that's quite a drop, isn't it? And wouldn't someone hear the splash?" Gavin asked in a low voice. He wasn't keen on the idea of literally jumping ship, even if they were very close to shore.

"We could climb down a rope and swim down to the far end of the docks."

"If you think it could be that simple for us to escape without being caught, then I agree."

"We're on the side of the ship facing away from the township. So long as no one comes back to the ship early, we'll be fine."

Marcas grabbed a long coil of rope and lashed it to one of the cannons. He latched the gun port hatch open and fed the rope through the square opening as quickly as he could while being sure the rope wouldn't tangle. Once the rope dangled down the side of the ship, Marcas peered through the gun port again. Seeing the coast was clear, he sent Gavin out first.

"I've never done anything like this before," Gavin sad softly as he headed out feet first. He was scared. Afraid of falling to the water, hurting himself, and making a huge splash. Afraid of someone peering down from the main deck and spotting him.

"Just take it slow," Marcas said, following Gavin out and down the side of the ship.

Gavin had a hard time not letting his hands slip against the coarse rope, and he knew they hadn't gone very far when his palms began smarting and burning. He forced himself to concentrate on taking it slowly, carefully, and not panicking. He wanted to ask Marcas if they could stop for a moment, just wait and recuperate, but he didn't dare speak for fear of someone up above hearing him. He wasn't certain it would be the best idea anyway with his arms and calves strained as they were.

After what seemed like a half hour, but was probably much less time, Gavin's shoes dipped into cool saltwater. Once submerged enough to let go of the rope and tread water, he moved away to give Marcas some room. The pirate joined him in the water and gestured in the direction he wanted to go.

Gavin hadn't been swimming for at least four years, and even then, it was never in the ocean. There was a lake near Auchencrow where the royal family sometimes summered. Memories of happier, worry-free times came rushing back to him. He could see Effie clearly in his mind's eye, laughing and splashing him. If he ever got home again, he'd be sure they had at least one more summer at the lake estate before she was married off and sent away to some other kingdom.

ONCE THEY'D SWUM around the *Crimson Wake*'s stern, Marcas made sure they kept close to the docks. There were a fair number of ships in port, and he was thankful for that. He couldn't help but look for his own ship, even with the knowledge it was just another tomb of the Deep.

Then he spotted a familiar ship, her faded green sails a beacon of hope. It was a sight he thought he'd never see again, and a welcome reminder that he wasn't as short on friends as he'd thought.

"C'mon. This way," he said to Gavin, who was behind him and off to his right.

By the time they pulled themselves up onto the pier where *The Jaded Jewel* was docked, they were both worn out, but Marcas ran up to his friend's ship with renewed energy. Jim was sure to help them out, and the old pirate would be ready to set sail as soon as he noticed the Crimson Queen shared the same port.

"Ahoy there, Jim!" Marcas called out. If he wasn't on his ship, Marcas would have to leave Gavin behind to go find him at one of the taverns. It was something he would only be willing to do as a last resort.

"Marcas, is that you?" A raspy voice called back a moment later. Then Jim appeared and gestured for Marcas to come aboard. "It is! Sink me; I can scarce believe my own eyes. Get up here, and bring your friend. You both look like you swam in!"

Marcas laughed as he and Gavin hurried on board the *Jewel* and were welcomed into the safety of the captain's cabin. Jim handed them a wool blanket each to dry off with.

"Please tell me I didn't just see her royal lunacy's ship moored down the docks," Jim said with a retiring sigh. He rubbed at his scarred throat and poured a round of drinks.

"Afraid it is, mate. And I hate to be the bearer of worse news, but me and Gavin have just scarpered without her noticing," Marcas said and prepared for his old friend to balk.

"Well, shit. No time for pleasantries then," Jim said and slammed his glass back down after a quick drink. Then he paused and got a good look at Gavin. "Your Highness! Captain Jimmy Balfour at your service, Sire."

Jim took his hat off, pressed it to his chest, and bowed.

"It's a pleasure to meet a friend of Marcas's," Gavin said with an awkward smile.

"Blimey, Marcas, on a first name basis with the prince of Crakesyde. You're full of surprises, mate!" Jim said with a laugh that turned into a cough. He dashed out of the cabin to gather his crew and set sail before Rhona caught wind of the pair of them having gone missing.

"You're sure we can trust him? Especially after he recognised me?" Gavin whispered once Jim had left them alone. He wasn't sure why he was whispering, but it made him feel more secure.

"I've been friends with Jimmy the Noose since I was a teenager. We sailed our ships together for about a year, probably the most lucrative year I ever had." Marcas took to more actively drying himself off. "Besides, he hates Rhona for double-crossing him. She's the reason for two of his trips to the gallows."

"Are you serious? That's *the* Jimmy the Noose? Hanged three times and he's still alive and well?" Gavin's jaw dropped. He'd never believed the stories about that particular pirate, thinking they were a creative exaggeration of the man cleverly avoiding the gallows at every turn. But he'd seen the marks on the man's neck; those scars could only have been created by one thing.

"The one and only." Marcas laughed. "You know a lot about famous pirates."

"Your lives are terribly interesting, but I can't believe half the stories anyway, thanks to embellishment." Gavin started to dry off more quickly as well. He didn't want to catch cold at sea. "And then there're some things that are left out. Like your being the Crimson Queen's brother. And how is it that you and your sister are so well spoken?"

"Old Angus had a tutor travel with us. He didn't want us to be uneducated just because we were pirates. He groomed us to be captains from the start."

"They don't mention that in the books I have. You'll be pleased to know they don't call you prince of the pirates either," Gavin said with a crooked grin.

The cabin door opened and Jim peered in. He nodded to both men in turn and then gestured behind him. "Found the rest of the crew lounging on the docks like a bunch of lubbers. We're about to set sail. Make yourselves comfortable, if you please."

"Any chance you're headed to Crakesyde?" Marcas asked.

"Not in my plans, no, but if Your Highness will forgive an old pirate his greed, for the promise of shiny compensation, we'd be glad to change our heading," Jim said.

"I'm sure my father would gladly reward whoever makes my safe return possible," Gavin said with a grateful nod.

"Aye, aye, Sire." Jim nodded and closed the door again.

CHAPTER 16

"So your mystery prisoner was the crown prince of Crakesyde?" Jim said, looking flabbergasted at the thought. He shook his head in disbelief.

Marcas was happy to have a drink with his old friend while Gavin slept in a hammock behind him. All that climbing and swimming had worn him out. Marcas would've liked to nap himself, but he wanted to be ready if his sister somehow figured out which ship he and Gavin were on and set out in pursuit of the *Jewel*.

"*Was* my prisoner being the key there," Marcas said and nodded once. He looked over his shoulder at Gavin. "Some days I think maybe my crew was right. That maybe redheads really are nothing but a lot of bad luck for a ship. But that would just be me blaming my own shortcomings on the nearest superstition."

"From what you've both said, you've been through a lot this past month, Marcas. I'm surprised to find you in one piece!" Jim gestured with his glass towards Gavin. "Not going to ransom him then?"

"Not a chance. And don't you get any ideas, you greedy old man," Marcas said with a laugh.

"Never! The lad's promised me gold as a reward. I'll just have to make him promise I can sail away with it too." Jim's cough of a laugh made him take another sip of his rum. "So what're you going to do after this great adventure comes to a close, mate? Find yourself a new ship? Retire?"

"I'm not sure," Marcas said and scratched his head. He had a few different ideas about what he might do once Gavin was safely home again—barring a trip to the gallows of course. There was no chance of retirement, because he had nothing to retire on. Buying a new ship was out of the question as well. That didn't mean he couldn't steal one, but he'd have to worry about doing that on his own, and he wasn't sure he could take on an entire crew alone and survive.

Quitting the pirating life was the most unappealing option for him, but unless he could happen upon some other outrageously grand scheme and pull it off, he wasn't sure it would even be worthwhile to continue. Then there was the nagging sense of discontent over leaving Gavin behind in Crakesyde, even if it was exactly where the prince belonged.

"I could always use an extra hand on the *Jewel*." Jim sounded too pitying for Marcas's pride to overlook.

"I appreciate the offer, but I'm too used to being in charge myself."

"Just know, whatever happens, the offer stands."

Marcas finished off what rum was in his glass. "I'm starting to believe I'm the worst pirate ever."

"Ever? That's a bit of a stretch," Jim said and shrugged. "You can't let a bit of bad luck colour the rest of your life. Ask me; I know from experience."

"Guess I'm still trying to crawl out from under my old man's shadow," Marcas said and smiled at his friend. Jim could afford the luxury of being constantly optimistic.

Marcas wasn't sure he'd reached rock bottom yet, so things could still get worse. He glanced over his shoulder at Gavin again and decided not to dwell on how much worse things could get.

"Deadeye was a strict captain, a superb marksman, and a cutthroat pirate to boot. It still took him decades to build his reputation, to blast his way to the top. I was friends with Angus before he became a stingy, arrogant recluse who wouldn't leave his own ship unless he was guaranteed to profit. Truth be told, I was fearing you'd started down that same road when we met up at Silverwell weeks ago."

"I've never really been in it for the profit, you know," Marcas said. That had always been Rhona's game—gold and jewels piled high. He smirked then, amused at his own nearly destitute situation. "Good thing too, since I've only got thirty gold pieces to my name."

"Gavin!" Marcas's voice filtered through a strange dream. At first, Gavin wasn't sure if he'd dreamt the voice itself, but then he felt Marcas's hand on his shoulder, shaking him back to the waking world. "Gavin, here. You said you knew how to use one of these. Jim couldn't stand to see you unarmed, and neither can I."

The hilt of a cutlass was shoved into his hand as he sat up in the hammock. He blinked up at Marcas, still groggy and not at all understanding what was going on.

"A duel, now?" he mumbled and shook his head, trying to gather his wits.

"Not one you'll like. The *Wake*'s after us. And gaining." Marcas walked back towards the open door to the captain's cabin and pulled it shut.

"Her crew is insanely large!" Gavin protested, his wits

returning to him. "We'll be outnumbered at least two to one. Possibly three!"

"I don't know that she'll broadside us, but I'm not about to underestimate the extent of her insanity. So long as she's not entirely sure we're even on board, Jim's crew ought to be relatively safe." Marcas ran a hand through his dark hair and paced up and down the little room. It was like watching him panic over his sister finding them at the island all over again.

"We just need to remain calm, that's all," Gavin said, sounding more confident than he felt. He knew himself too well. He was a veritable coward when it came to the potential of being hurt or killed. A duel he could handle, happily, but a duel between gentlemen was for sport, not survival.

"Doesn't matter how calm we are; they'll find us in here once they've caught the *Jewel*," Marcas said. "We can't get below decks without a chance of being spotted. Rhona's addicted to using that sodding spyglass of hers. She's always trying to make up for her lost eye. At least she can't aim for shit."

Gavin sat heavily on the settee and stared up at the ceiling. He couldn't stand watching Marcas pace furiously *and* carry on a conversation with himself. It only served to make his own panicked emotions rise to the surface.

This could be it. The end. Of his life, or Marcas's, or both. Captain Jimmy's crew wasn't likely to come out of a confrontation with the queen's men unscathed either. Gavin wasn't ready to face those sorts of possibilities head-on. Even with a sword in hand he felt feeble.

"How can the *Wake* go faster than the *Jewel*? The *Jewel*'s a smaller ship!" Gavin said, frustrated with the turn of events.

"She's an old Highbronian navy ship, was one of the fastest in her fleet. Designed for speed so she could overtake any other ship, no matter the size." Marcas finally stopped pacing and sat down next to Gavin. He slouched low on the settee and put his head in his hands. "This can't be all there is left."

"Waiting to be recaptured?" Gavin sighed and rubbed the sleep from his eyes.

"Hoping my sister doesn't forget she loves me."

"I can't honestly believe she'd ever kill you," Gavin said in a quiet voice. In reality, he wasn't sure how far her insane logic would take her. She might have seen Marcas's escape from the ship as mutinous and to be punished with death. Then again, she took Morris in without any qualms. However, she might still see fit to punish him, or likely both of them, with her cat o' nine tails. He put a hand over Marcas's and laced their fingers together.

"I'd sooner die myself than let anything happen to you," Marcas said.

Gavin gazed into his green eyes. For that moment, all of his fears quieted in his mind, and he felt safe knowing Marcas would watch his back. Instantly he knew he'd do the same for Marcas. The sword fell out of his hand and clattered to the wood floor. He wrapped his arms around Marcas as best he could, slid closer, and their lips came crashing down on one another. The kisses were frantic, hurried, because neither one knew if they'd be able to enjoy the comfort and safety of one another's arms again.

CHAPTER 17

THE CREW BEGAN SHOUTING OUTSIDE THE CAPTAIN'S CABIN. Marcas focused on Jim's rasping voice barking out commands. They weren't taking true evasive manoeuvres to avoid undue suspicion. Jim had enough personal reasons to try to outrun the *Crimson Wake*, but he'd warned Marcas as soon as the *Wake* had been sighted that he would slow down and allow Rhona to board if she bothered to hail *The Jaded Jewel*.

He broke away from Gavin reluctantly, but was glad to see him take up his dropped cutlass and give it a few practice swings.

"I'm used to a rapier, a piercing blade, not one meant for slashing, but I'll be able to defend myself," Gavin said. His voice lacked confidence.

"Just remember, this isn't some fencing lesson. If we have to fight, we're fighting for our lives. That means you need to strike to kill."

Gavin stopped his duel with an imaginary foe and stared at Marcas with a horrified expression. "I've never killed a man before."

"It's a dirty business, taking lives, but it's your opponent's life or your own. If you're not ready to end his life, he'll be ready to end yours." Marcas remembered his own reaction the first time he'd taken another human being's life. His sister had cheered, clapped him on the back, and congratulated him on becoming a man. He still didn't think there was anything wonderful about killing, even if it was in self-defence. His father had been more sober about the event, but in the aftermath had been glad his son was still alive and capable of taking care of himself. He'd been fifteen. Now it was as much a part of life for him as he supposed it should have been. Another harsh reality that was difficult to face at first.

"I don't hear any cannons firing or grenades," Gavin said.

"Could be Jim and Rhona are chatting. I can hear some kind of shouting going on." Marcas stood up and took a few steps closer to the cabin door. There was a window in it, but it was covered with a small curtain. It was old smoky glass anyway, not good for spying out of. He listened carefully but couldn't make out what words were being exchanged. They were too far away from the cabin now, most likely at midship.

The sudden sound of grenades exploding on deck caused Marcas to jump back from the door. He drew one of his freshly loaded pistols and cocked it. The *Wake*'s crew had taken the first shots after all. Marcas was sorry he'd dragged Jim into this.

The *Jewel* lurched, and Marcas had to steady himself against the wall. That meant the grappling irons had been sent across and the *Wake*'s crew were lashing the ships together. Routine let Marcas guess what the next few steps might be, but since this was a personal affront to the queen herself, he wouldn't be surprised if Rhona and Arreid crossed the breach ahead of the boarding party.

He forced himself to wait, to not barrel out of the cabin before he could better assess the situation. Not that he was sure who he'd threaten with his pistol. He couldn't shoot his own sister. Arreid was fair game though, and so were the rest of her crew. If he saw that traitorous maggot Morris, he'd have his target chosen for him.

～

"Where are they?!" Rhona bellowed in Jimmy the Noose's leathery crease-lined face. She had a good hold of the collar of his shirt and wasn't about to let go until she had an answer. "I know you're hiding them, Jimmy boy! Yours was the only ship to leave just after we docked!"

"I already told you three times I haven't seen Marcas in nearly a month," Jimmy shot back hoarsely.

Rhona released him, half shoving him away from herself. She glared at him, her top lip curling in anger. "Search this entire ship!" she shrieked at her crew, rounding on them and flailing her hands at the *Jewel*. "Turn it inside out! Just find my brother and my fiancé, and bring them back to me in one piece!"

She didn't believe Jimmy any further than she could have thrown him. He'd been one of her main rivals when she'd first started out on her own, but only because he'd abandoned his friendship with her father just before he'd been killed. A part of her could never let that go. If he'd been there, a true friend, her father might have survived his final battle. It might not have made a difference, and the Noose hadn't had a direct hand in Angus's end, but it made no difference to Rhona. Anyone who would turn their back on her father—and that was exactly what Jimmy going off to captain his own ship had been—was an enemy. She'd made sure Jimmy knew she hated him. If only he'd died when he was supposed to!

"I don't want your crew stealing any of my cargo. Every last barrel of gunpowder better be where it's meant to be when they're through!" Jimmy said as he watched some of the *Wake*'s men head below decks. He followed them, seeming agitated with the idea of them going down there.

"You there!" Rhona gestured to two of her men who were about to open the captain's cabin door. "Head down below with the rest. We'll rifle through his personal effects last."

Jimmy might have been good at escaping the gallows, but he'd never been terribly bright in Rhona's opinion. He was a terrible gambler, which was why he never had much gold for very long. His crew seemed just as lazy now as the last time she'd run into the *Jewel*, so it was obvious to Rhona that Jimmy was hiding her brother and the prince with his precious cargo.

"What should we do with him, My Queen? He might get in the way," Arreid said softly to her.

Rhona stroked his arm with her ring-laden hand and grinned up at him. "Be a dear and tie him up for me."

MARCAS HEARD Jim shouting obscenities and cursing Rhona's existence. Something wasn't going right, and he'd had enough waiting around. He gestured for Gavin to stay back, hidden around the corner from sight of the door at least. Then he threw the door open and marched out on the deck. His target was easy to spot, and he aimed his pistol up at Arreid's head.

"Rhona, get back on your ship or your first mate gets his brains blown out," Marcas commanded. He took a few seconds to take in his surroundings. Jim's crew was scattered, and the few men on deck were Rhona's—easy to spot thanks to their red sashes. A glance to his left and he saw Jim bound at the wrists and being tied to the mizzenmast by Morris and some woman from the *Wake*.

Rhona bounded over to her brother. A grin split her face, and she held her arms out in a plea for a hug. Marcas wasn't having it for once in his life.

"My darling brother! You're safe! And where's my fiancé? You don't think I missed the part where you kidnapped him. Again." Rhona waggled her finger at him like a disappointed mother.

"He's fine; that's all you need know. Now do as I asked. Your next words had better be a command for your men to return to your ship, or it's death for your first mate." He wouldn't ask her again, and he hoped, for her sake, she realised just how serious he was. There was little hope that what sway he had over her would hold for very long or take them very far. She had a way of turning everything he said or did around on him. He glanced at Arreid to ensure he wasn't trying anything funny.

"Marcas, you know I can't do that. I have to teach Jimmy boy a lesson for lying to his queen," Rhona said.

Half a second to check his aim, and he pulled the trigger. The ball fired from Marcas's pistol forced its way through Arreid's skull above his right eye. The first mate crumpled to the deck in a heap, and Rhona rushed to his side, shrieking his name before Marcas had a chance to holster his weapon.

"I warned you," Marcas said, his voice full of scorn. He didn't want to imagine what his sister was feeling then. It was almost too much to watch her cradle the dead man's head while stroking his cheek, oblivious to all the blood. She whimpered and tears ran down her face. For a moment, it was their father's death all over again. That meant her rage was merely building until it reached the boiling point.

"*Arreid...* How could you?" she whispered as she stood. Eye on her brother, glaring at him with pure hatred, she shrieked at the top of her lungs and drew her sword. "You bastard!"

Marcas drew his sword before she charged. Her every thrust and swing was erratic, as if she were flailing instead of attempting to hit him. As soon as he thought he might still have brotherly immunity, Rhona feigned left and slashed right, catching Marcas's upper arm with her blade.

"Look what you've made me do!" she cried and thrust her sword at him angrily. She allowed herself to be overrun by her emotions, but Marcas caught her sloppy footwork. A quick parry by Marcas and bold step forward cost Rhona her balance. She fell backwards and landed hard on the deck. Her sword slipped from her grasp and clattered to the deck a few feet away from her.

"If you'd just left, this wouldn't have happened!" Marcas tried to keep his own temper in check, but years of letting his sister push him around and walk all over him without more than a grumbled protest made it difficult. He didn't want to physically hurt her, even if she had given him a good cut already. That didn't mean it was easy to shove aside the fact that she'd burned his ship. Burned his crew—the very men and women who'd been like a family to them for over twenty years. "Get back on the *Wake* and sail her away!"

"What're you bilge rats standing around slack jawed for?!" she shouted at her crew. It was obviously not her idea of fun to be unarmed in the middle of a duel. "Tie him up!"

Five of the *Wake*'s crew drew their swords and crept towards Marcas. He felt marginally lucky none of them were foolish enough to draw a pistol on him. They were well aware their queen would flay anyone who killed her brother.

"Two against six is better odds, don't you agree?" Gavin

said as he hurried over to stand beside Marcas, borrowed sword at the ready.

"You're a madman!" Marcas growled. He wasn't happy with Gavin exposing himself to danger. Any one of the *Wake*'s crew could've fired on him as soon as he'd stepped out of the captain's cabin, but their queen had an obvious fiscal attachment to Gavin. Whoever was fool enough to harm him would have to worry about facing her wrath later. Perhaps Gavin had more of a tactical mind than Marcas had given him credit for.

That didn't stop the pirates from encroaching. Marcas kept his eyes on his sister, making sure she didn't try to reach for her sword or whatever other weapons she might've had hidden under her longcoat. One of the pirates lunged at Gavin, and in the split second it took Marcas to glance up and see Gavin really was a good swordsman, Rhona rolled to the side and grabbed her sword.

She jumped to her feet and slashed wildly at Marcas again. He stepped back, leaning side to side and parrying frantically with his own blade to avoid her blows. He knew if he could get her back on the defensive she'd leave herself open again.

"Marcas!" Gavin's voice was desperate. He'd been overpowered by the other pirates, and they rushed to tie him up.

Without warning, Rhona punched Marcas squarely on his jaw. Her rings scraped across his cheek, but he didn't have time to feel for blood. He swung on her, missed narrowly as she leaned out of the way, dropped her sword, and lunged at him, knocking him flat on the deck. Rhona's hands wrapped tightly around Marcas's neck, and he wasn't sure if she'd let go until he stopped breathing.

"How could you take him away from me? How could you?" she forced the words out through her teeth.

Marcas pried at her hands, fingers scrabbling against the

sharp edges of her gem-encrusted rings without gaining purchase. She was strong; she always had been, and now with her fuel of rage she banged his head against the deck, shaking him furiously. Gasping for breath, throat flexing painfully under her tightening grip, Marcas felt pressure build in his head and desperate lungs.

He went for his loaded pistol. He had to get it free and cocked before she killed him. *Kill or be killed*. What fate would Gavin face if he didn't survive? He freed the gun of its holster, but his fingers didn't want to work anymore as he strained impossibly for air.

Rhona snatched the pistol out of Marcas's hand. He sucked in a breath of air as she smacked him over the head with the butt of his own gun.

CHAPTER 18

GAVIN THOUGHT HE COULD HAVE HANDLED BEING TIED TO THE main mast of the *Jewel* as though he were hugging it if he were still wearing his shirt. It was humiliating enough to be trussed up like some criminal, but to be roughly stripped of his dignity was too much.

He hoped the queen talked herself hoarse before she wielded the cruel-looking cat o' nine tails cradled in her hands. Even though he could barely see Marcas standing behind him out of the corner of his eye, it somehow made the entire situation worse knowing he was there and unable to help. The queen had tied Marcas's hands behind his back and taken his weapons from him as soon as she'd knocked him out.

"Marcas, dearest baby brother," the queen said while slapping her cat against the palm of her hand. "I can't take your lover from you like you took mine. Arreid. If only Gavin here weren't so important to my dream of a true pirate empire, I'd cut his pretty little head off while you watched!"

"Leave him alone. It's me who's killed your lapdog. It was me who kidnapped your fiancé and ran off." Marcas struggled against the pirates holding him. "You know you want to do more than give me some weak cut and half-arsed strangling!"

"You're exactly right, darling brother," she said, her voice hard and cold. "Which is exactly why I'm going to make His Royal Highness bleed and cry and beg me to stop. Because watching him in pain, in agony, and wishing I'd end his pathetic existence instead of strike him again? *That* will hurt you more than *I* ever could."

"That's complete nonsense, and you know it," Marcas spat the words out with contention. "I can't feel his pain for him."

The queen grabbed Marcas by the chin and looked him in the eye.

"You always were a rotten liar, Marcas," she said and kissed him on the forehead. She marched over to Gavin, which made him struggle with renewed fervour against the ropes holding him to the main mast.

Sharp stings cut through Gavin's back as the queen swung her cat. He flinched—he couldn't help it—and the next lash came much quicker than he expected. He gritted his teeth and clamped his eyes tightly shut. Each successive lashing brought more pain with it. His raw skin prickled as the cat's leather tails whipped across it over and over again. Gavin bit his lip to keep from making more than tiny, choked grunts. He had no hope she'd stop before she made him bleed.

"Stop! Rhona, leave him alone!" Marcas bellowed.

"I'm captain here!" she shrieked back and struck Gavin three more times in rapid succession. "I give the commands!"

The stinging pain dulled to a burn, but she struck Gavin again. Tears welled in his eyes as he finally cried out. He'd never experienced so much physical pain in his life.

"Let the boy be, you bilge-brained bitch!" Jimmy the Noose's rasp carried over the deck.

Suddenly the lashings stopped. Gavin breathed in sobbing gasps.

"I've had enough for one day! This is too much bloody trouble! Redheads! Should've listened!" the queen screamed like a child throwing a tantrum. "Let Marcas alone and prepare the *Jewel*'s former captain to kiss the bottom of my ship! That bastard can't escape death forever! And I'll have something to bring me joy today!"

"No!" Marcas shouted, but his protest went unheeded.

"Have fun with your new ship, Marcas. My gift to you even though we all know you don't deserve it. You're a shit pirate and a worse brother! And if I see you again after today, I might not be feeling so generous," the queen called out as she followed her men back onto the *Crimson Wake*.

MARCAS WASTED no time making sure Gavin was all right. Luckily, Rhona hadn't taken the opportunity to break open the skin on his back, but that didn't mean Gavin wasn't going to be in pain for days. Marcas turned around and leaned forward so his hands could reach the knots at Gavin's wrists. It was strange having to undo a knot backwards and without looking.

"I thought she was going to kill you," Gavin said weakly.

"So did I," Marcas said. He'd believed Rhona when she'd said she'd not be feeling generous next time. At least she'd no longer be hunting him down like she had been for the last few years, so they were less likely to run into one another.

"Why hasn't Jimmy's crew come to help us?"

"They're locked below decks, I think." Marcas wasn't sure what had happened to the crew after the ship had been searched. He'd been preoccupied. "We'll get them out next. We've got to try to help Jim."

"You don't think... She's not going to set the *Jewel* on fire, is she?"

Marcas didn't reply because he wasn't sure. He worked the knot faster. Soon he freed Gavin's left arm, and Gavin was able to untie Marcas's hands. Both freed of their restraints, they went to release the *Jewel*'s crew. The hatch was held shut by a heavy barrel, and the pair worked it off to one side before Marcas hefted the hatch wide open.

"They've gone back to the *Wake*, but they've got Captain Jim," he told the crew as they rushed out onto the deck. "We've got to do something to save him before he's keelhauled."

"We ain't got to do nothin' but save our own hides, beggin' your pardon," one of the sailors said. The crew fell about to their usual posts and got the *Jewel* ready to set sail.

"You're just going to leave your captain to die?" Marcas asked.

"In case of hostilities we're to keep loyal to the *Jewel* and what crew can steer her out of harm's way. It's in the articles, it is. You can see 'em fer yerself in the captain's cabin," the pirate said somewhat sadly.

"And I suppose you're the new captain then?" Marcas didn't have to see the articles to know that much was true. Jim had always been one to follow the old school of pirates.

"Nah. We'll take a vote once we're clear o' the *Wake*," the pirate said, going off to help some of the other crew members cut the ropes lashing the two ships together.

A loud, high-pitched cackle that could only belong to Rhona sounded from the other ship. Marcas heard her ordering her crew, but couldn't make out the words themselves. He guessed it was the command to scrape his old friend along the bottom of the *Wake*. Jim's last voyage at sea. A splash confirmed his fears, and he raced to the rails of the *Jewel* to see if he could make out some other cause of the disturbance in the water. There was no such luck. A long line of rope trailed off the stern of the boat and into the water. Another barking command from his sister and the rope went taut against the ship. He tore his eyes away, knowing what would happen next.

Gavin put a hand on his shoulder.

"He saved my neck, and I couldn't do a bloody thing to save his," Marcas said and smacked his fists against the *Jewel*'s railing.

"If you'd have really tried, his help would have been in vain," Gavin said.

The words rang true but didn't make the loss of his friend any easier. Jim was a good man, a great friend, and ten times the pirate Marcas would ever be.

He looked up again to see the gap between the two ships grow slowly but surely. If he'd have tried jumping across before Jim had been dumped in the water, he would have chanced falling and being smashed between the hulls.

"Do you think he'd mind if I borrowed a shirt?" Gavin asked sheepishly.

Marcas looked at him and pulled him into an embrace, careful to keep his arms around Gavin's hips to avoid touching the area of his back that had been subjected to the cat. "You probably won't want to wear one for a day or two. It'll hurt."

Gavin kissed the side of Marcas's neck. "Please don't think this is your fault."

"But it is my fault. Everything that's happened to you since you left home has been because I attacked the *Maiden Fair*," Marcas said soberly. He was under no delusions, even if Gavin wanted to save him some grief. It had been a poor venture aside from the tipoff about the king's "diplomat." The *Maiden Fair* hadn't even been carrying any cargo besides the supplies they'd needed for their voyage to Crakesyde. It was the last decent act of piracy he'd done in months but had been a complete failure in the end.

"If you hadn't attacked the *Maiden Fair*, I never would have met you," Gavin said, his voice still quiet and remarkably calm. He kissed Marcas on the cheek, then on the lips. A lingering kiss, a moment of happiness in a sea of ill fortune.

"Look at that!" one of the crew members shouted, awed.

"The evil witch deserves it! Hope it tears her ship apart an' her with it!" another said with a cold laugh.

Marcas and Gavin both turned to look back at the *Crimson Wake*. A shark's fin the size of a house circled the large ship. The monster attached to it had to have been nearly as long as the *Wake* herself.

"Can that... Will it attack a ship?" Gavin asked.

"That's the danger of keelhauling. Only the mad and the foolish do it anymore. All that blood has a chance of calling up something from the deep. A squid, a serpent, or a shark," Marcas said, his voice flat.

They couldn't do anything but watch as the *Wake*'s crew fired muskets and pistols at the enormous creature. The projectiles only angered the shark, and it rammed against the ship so hard she shook.

The *Jewel*'s crew, on the other hand, were much more interested in better catching what little wind was to be had and getting as far away from the shark, and the *Wake*, as possible. Where there was one, there were more.

Marcas couldn't tear his eyes away. The shark rammed the ship again. The *Wake* rocked so hard a few pirates fell overboard. A frenzy of motion churned the water; then the shark knocked the ship around again. Soon a second great fin appeared, larger than the first, and headed straight for the *Wake*. Instead of ramming the ship, the shark's great grey nose peaked out of the sea and bit the rudder, splintering it to pieces. The *Wake*'s crew fired more shots at the beasts, but it was useless. The sharks would tear the ship apart until their hunger was sated.

"What's that?" Gavin pointed to a dark, sinuous streak curving through the water in the distance like a snake through grass. It disappeared as quickly as it appeared, but there was no mistaking the movements of a sea drake.

"It's my father's namesake," Marcas said softly. He'd only seen drakes a handful of times—he'd encountered sharks far more often—but every time, he felt nothing but cold, powerless dread.

A massive, black head lined with indigo fins rose out of the water with a struggling shark in its maw. Blood poured out of the injured fish, staining the frothing sea around the *Wake*. Cannons fired. The drake dropped the huge shark onto the ship and let out a terrifying trilling roar.

Marcas couldn't watch anymore. He turned round and strode away, swaying with the *Jewel*, unsure whether or not he could retire in the captain's cabin. Gavin was right behind him, but he couldn't bear to glance back at him towards the chaos. They were lucky enough to have their distance from the *Wake* steadily growing, with nothing more than rough seas as a consequence.

"What's your heading?" Marcas asked one of the other pirates.

"Away from 'ere!" one replied loudly from across the deck.

"And after that?" He'd be persistent until he got a real answer.

"Got to stop at Morbryde again, I s'pose," another pirate said.

"Not if we're headin' north like Captain Jim says we would!" a third piped up, distraught.

"Captain Jim's dead if ye haven't eyes in yer head to be seein' that with!" the first shouted.

The bickering continued, and Marcas massaged his temples. They wouldn't be able to make it to port before voting on a captain. They'd end up sailing "away" until they ran out of supplies.

"Stow your gab, mates!" Marcas commanded. The arguments ceased. "If there's no objection, I wouldn't mind acting as your captain until we reach the next port. I'll gladly honour whatever articles Jim had set for this cruise."

Heads turned, looking amongst one another, but no one did more than shrug.

"Does anyone know why Jim wanted to head north?" Marcas asked.

"Captain Jim wanted to rove the 'Ighbron isles, sir. We 'adn't done them since our last cruise. Fig'red they'd be ripe again, sir," one of the men closest to Marcas replied.

"Then let's change our heading. We'll follow through with Captain Jim's last plan."

CHAPTER 19

GAVIN WAS GLAD TO BE ABLE TO RELAX ON THE CHAISE lounge in the captain's cabin. He had trouble finding a comfortable position, but half curled on his side with his back facing the rest of the room seemed to be the perfect arrangement. He could hear the sounds of Marcas trying to drown himself in gulp after gulp of rum from the late captain's private stock, belching intermittently. Strangely, he didn't feel the least bit worried about where they were going, because he wasn't sure where he should end up anymore.

If he returned home, his father would dismiss his harrowing journey as a young man's lark and have Marcas arrested and then hanged. If he went to Highbron looking like some filthy nobody, no one would believe he was the Prince of Crakesyde. Pirates might have been eager to believe him, but royal guards and nobles would require more proof than a coin comparison. Any beggar might look like a king. Even if they did believe him, they might recognise the *Jewel* as a pirate ship and have Marcas and the other men arrested and condemned to death. No matter what their line of work, the *Jewel*'s crew were obviously good men. As was Marcas.

He was certain, however, that he didn't want to go anywhere without Marcas by his side. There was no doubt in his mind they'd both be dead by now if they hadn't stuck together. He wondered if they couldn't pretend the *Jewel* was a legitimate merchant ship when they arrived at Highbron. Marcas could easily pass for a fellow courtier so long as he was sober and didn't start cursing. They would both need new clothes, especially if he wanted Marcas to come off as upper class.

The charade played out so well in Gavin's mind as he drifted off to sleep that he dreamed he was meeting the Highbronian royalty with Marcas as his companion. Everyone was fooled until King Malcolm showed up and cowed his fellow royals for not being able to spot a pirate when they saw one.

"It's a bad dream. It's all right, Gavin," Marcas said, his hand resting warmly on Gavin's arm.

"I dreamt we were arrested." Gavin flinched in pain, realizing he'd rolled onto his back as he slept, and pushed himself up into a sitting position. He rubbed his eyes with the palms of his hands and ran his fingers through his hair. "Must've been tossing and turning."

"I had to make sure you didn't roll right off the chaise," Marcas said and plopped down next to him. He offered the bottle of rum, now half empty, though there was no telling how much had been in it when he'd begun.

Gavin graciously accepted and took a good swig before handing the bottle back. "I had this grand idea for how I could complete my mission without you being hanged."

"I have to hear this," Marcas said with a grin.

"We'd have to buy or steal something a courtier would wear. Two courtiers, in fact," Gavin said. He leaned over onto

Marcas as he explained his scheme, convinced the idea was flawless. It had to work.

When Gavin was done explaining, Marcas burst out laughing.

"What's so funny about that? It's a good idea," Gavin said defensively. He sat up straight again and cringed at how tight and painful the skin between his shoulder blades had become.

"You're so sure that a king, of all people, would believe I'm some fancy-pants courtier?" Marcas spluttered; then his laughter was renewed.

"So long as you don't have anything to drink and are dressed the part, I don't see how anyone could think otherwise," Gavin said.

"You're thinking like a pirate now! Planning to steal and lie. To royalty no less!" Marcas was too amused at the idea for Gavin's liking.

"Let's hear your brilliant idea for how I'm supposed to get my sister a husband and make my father proud of me for once in my life? And all without getting you hanged!" Gavin stood up stiffly, walked across the room, and sat at the end of the bed. It was the same sort of bed they'd shared on the *Crimson Wake*, but he wasn't concerned with any of that now. He just wanted Marcas to help him, not laugh in his face.

"I didn't mean it like that, Gavin." Marcas set the bottle of rum on the floor near the chaise lounge, walked over to the bed, and sat down beside Gavin. "I don't know what we can do. We might not even be able to stay with the *Jewel* after they've elected a new captain. I'm hoping we'll be able to book passage with another ship that's headed to Highbron's mainland if that's the case."

"What will you do while I'm stuck entertaining the prince and king for a fortnight, possibly longer? Hang around the docks and drink away what little money you have left?"

Gavin couldn't keep the sarcasm from his voice. Too much had happened for one day, and too much still hung over his head. Things that only he could accomplish.

"I'll wait for you," Marcas said with a shrug. He took his weapons off and set them on the floor by his feet; then his boots came off, and he flopped back onto the bed.

"There's too much of a chance you'll be recognised and hanged. We've gone through too much trouble to save your neck repeatedly for you to die just so I can finish this ridiculous mission."

"So do you want to do this job or not?" Marcas asked.

Gavin didn't respond right away. It all boiled down to just that again: he didn't know what he wanted to do. He knew he wanted to see his sister once more, to let her know he was all right and tell her about his madcap adventures at sea. Of course he knew he wanted to be with Marcas, too, but Gavin couldn't puzzle out how to do both.

"All right, love?" Marcas asked quietly. He patted the mattress beside him.

"No, I'm not." Gavin sighed and kicked his shoes off. He crawled up the bed and lay down half on top of Marcas, half on the blanket covering the mattress. "What are we going to do? Where will we go?"

"Back to the island?" Marcas suggested with a smirk. He closed his eyes and seemed contented just to be so close to Gavin.

"We don't know where it is," Gavin said. He knew he wouldn't be ready to go back there unless he was sure he could get word to his sister, somehow, that he was alive.

"Do we have to think about tomorrow?" Marcas sounded extremely tired.

Gavin couldn't blame him. He was sure the only reasons he felt so wide awake were the myriad thoughts running through his mind. He kissed Marcas's stubbled neck. "We'll need our rest."

～

DAYS PASSED SMOOTHLY with no sign of the *Wake* following them, and Marcas was glad the *Jewel*'s crew had been willing to allow him to be their temporary captain. It felt good to be at the helm of a ship again, even momentarily, and he hated not being in charge when he was at sea. There were too many perks involved with being the captain to make him want to be anything else. It helped to take his mind off Jim's fate and speculation about what had happened to Rhona after her ship had faded from view.

His mind was too wont to wander into horrible death scenarios when survival of any of the *Wake*'s crew had looked so dismal. If she'd survived on a rowboat or hunk of ship flotsam, she would've been sure to face death from exposure, dehydration, or starvation. All options lead to a grisly end.

He and Gavin discussed various ways to get to the Highbronian capital city of Hroldergate but hadn't settled on any one plan yet. Marcas couldn't help feeling Gavin was only trying to carry on with the mission his father gave him out of his sense of loyalty to his family. If he truly wanted to carry out the task, he wouldn't be so confused about what to do now that he was free of the Crimson Queen.

Marcas wasn't sure what he was going to do once they made port either. He could sign up as a crew member of some other pirate ship, but that wouldn't do anything for his reputation. There was also the annoyance of having to work his way back up to the top. In his mind, the island looked more and more inviting. So long as he could have Gavin there with him, he thought he might be happy to retire. Maybe he could pretend to be dead? Then everyone would be left to wonder whatever happened to Captain Drake.

Later in the day, he checked some of the maps Jim had left neatly folded in the trunk by his bed. Most of them were more detailed and of better quality than the ones Marcas used to have on the *Ebon Drake*. For a moment, he entertained the idea that shoddy maps were what had cost him so much, but even then, he knew he was the one to blame.

Unfortunately, many of the Highbronian colonies were large, well-established cities, which meant a smaller carrack like the *Jaded Jewel* would be better off avoiding them. The Crakesydian navy might have been relegated to cruising Crakesyde's own borders for the last few years, but the Highbronians were smart enough to send war ships to protect its colonies. Even the handful of poor Engothian fishing villages were privy to the protection of Highbron's navy, thanks to an accord struck ten years prior. The *Jewel* would be more likely to find a lucrative bit of piracy near some of the more southerly isles that had newer and smaller colonial ports.

"Ship off larboard side!" one of the crew called out for all to hear.

Marcas furrowed his brow and left the maps behind as he walked through the open cabin doors onto the main deck. Gavin met him at the rails overlooking the side of the ship and handed him a borrowed spyglass.

"They're headed straight for us, but it's not the *Wake*. The sails are white," Gavin said.

It was a medium-sized ship, but a fast one. Marcas could tell, even while looking at it through the spyglass, the other ship was gaining on them. The wind hadn't been in the *Jewel*'s favour since they'd left Morbryde, so the carrack sailed slowly on her way. Then Marcas spotted what was giving the other ship the advantage: huge oars stuck out of the sides of the ship, propelling it onward.

"They're using sweeps," Marcas said. He handed the spyglass back to Gavin and turned to face the crew. He called out so all hands on deck could hear him. "They've got sweeps! Could be a Highbronian navy vessel! We can't outrace them with hardly any wind in our sails. Keep your wits about you!"

"What if they fire on us?" Gavin sounded panicked.

"Then we'll fire back," Marcas said.

Half an hour later, the other ship moved within hailing distance. They flew the brown and gold Highbronian flag, emblazoned with a white dragon at the centre. Another look through the spyglass at the uniformed sailors on deck told Marcas it was, indeed, a royal navy ship. He remembered the ransom letter then, and knew it was entirely possible he would be arrested before this encounter was over.

"Ahoy there! What's your business in Highbronian waters?" a sailor called from the Highbronian ship.

"Selling goods," Marcas called back, one hand cupped over the side of his mouth.

"What's your cargo?" the sailor replied.

"Gunpowder," Marcas called back again. It was the truth, and hopefully, it would keep them from being foolhardy enough to fire the great guns on them if a skirmish broke out.

"Prepare to be boarded by Captain Hurst of His Majesty, King Redmond of Highbron's royal navy! Failure to comply will lead to the arrest of your officers for contempt of the crown!"

Marcas tucked the spyglass into one of the pockets of his coat and called out the command for his crew to slow the *Jewel* while the navy ship manoeuvred into position to send across their boarding party.

"Is this normal? What are we supposed to do? Pretend to be a legitimate merchant operation?" Gavin asked Marcas.

"This is procedure. The commanding officer will come aboard with a small party, he'll ask me a few questions about where we're headed, where we've come from, that sort of thing, and if he gets the faintest hint we're not legitimate merchants, we'll be clapped in irons," Marcas said, hands clasped behind his back. He had to appear unconcerned, and it obviously bothered Gavin that he wasn't outwardly alarmed.

"There's no way we can pull this off!" Gavin said. He ran a hand through his hair in frustration.

"This is your ticket to Highbron, then home again, Gavin," Marcas said, his eyes still on the navy ship as it made its approach. He didn't want to look at Gavin just then. Knowing he was going to be arrested was bad enough, but knowing he couldn't accompany Gavin for the rest of his journey made the entire situation worse. His insides were awash in turmoil, counter to the confidence he had to project. This wasn't the way he'd wanted or expected things to go, not really, but a part of him understood it was for the best. He'd spent his life doing terrible things, and now he was reaping the just rewards. Gavin, on the other hand, would be returned to his world of safety and security, better able to lead his people with the knowledge he'd gained at sea. Just because it was the right way didn't mean Marcas had to like it.

"They'll never believe I'm…me!" Gavin said, holding his hands up in defeat and then letting them drop at his sides again. He took a deep breath and watched the navy ship as well.

CHAPTER 20

Gavin's mind raced as Captain Hurst and his men boarded the *Jewel* and began questioning Marcas. He had no idea what he could say to the man to convince him he was the crown prince of Crakesyde. He didn't have his signet ring with him because his father had ordered him to leave it at home. It was a way for people to quickly and easily recognise him as royalty, so of course a mere diplomat wouldn't have it. Now, more than ever, Gavin was convinced his father sent him out in the world to get killed. If he hadn't known Marcas had happened upon the *Maiden Fair* by chance, he would have guessed his father had hired the pirate ship to do the kidnapping himself.

"Cabin boy," he heard Marcas say to Hurst. He looked over and saw him pointing in his direction with a smirk on his face.

Gavin thought that was awfully brave and possibly stupid.

"A little old to be a cabin boy, aren't you?" Captain Hurst said, his voice deep. He turned and addressed Gavin.

The man was intimidatingly tall and broad chested, his eyes a lighter shade of brown than his skin, which bore traditional Highbronian sailing tattoos of curling waves up the sides of his neck and over the backs of his large hands. Gavin found he couldn't think of how to properly reply.

"Me? Oh, er, I'm eighteen, sir," he stammered. He tried to remind himself that the military was on his side, but he was unconvinced the captain would see things that way. Gavin glanced at Marcas nervously, then back up at Hurst, who scrutinised him with narrowed eyes.

"Do you have a name, cabin boy?" Hurst asked.

"Gavin, sir." Another glance at Marcas, whose face was unreadable, then back at the captain so as not to be disrespectful.

"And how long have you been sailing on the *Jilted Jewel*, Gavin?"

Gavin furrowed his brows. Marcas must have given the captain a false ship name while Gavin had been lost in his own worried thoughts. How long *had* they been on board? Five days? Eight? If he contradicted Marcas, the captain would immediately know something was amiss. Or that Gavin was completely daft.

"A week, I think, sir," he said. It was a guess, a bad one, but he hoped Captain Hurst would think he just had a bad memory.

The discerning look the captain gave Marcas dashed that hope. "I see. And how long have you been sailing with Captain MacLeod?"

"Er...nearly two months, I'd say," Gavin said slowly, his eyes flicking back to Marcas again. He wanted to mention they'd been attacked by the Crimson Queen but thought it would be too much information.

Hurst nodded to one of the sailors standing to his right. She handed some papers to the captain. He shuffled through them until he found the ones he was looking for and glanced from the papers to Gavin, then to Marcas.

"Something the matter, sir?" Marcas asked, sounding almost patronizing.

Hurst held the papers up and turned them around for Marcas and his crew to see. One was a sketch of Marcas: a wanted poster. The other was a sketch of Gavin. He recognised the pose and serious expression from one of the portraits he'd sat for with Effie when he'd been sixteen.

"Handsome fellows, sir," Marcas said, grinning broadly.

"Of course you'd think so, Captain *Drake*," Hurst said, his tone sharp. "Clap him in irons and take the crown prince on board. Get him something warm to eat and some fresh clothes."

Without so much as a salute, the sailors began to carry out their orders. Gavin was shocked. How had they known to look for him? How had they even known he was with Marcas? The two sailors escorting him towards the navy ship didn't say anything. He turned his head and watched as Marcas allowed himself to be handcuffed without bothering to put up a fight.

"No!" Gavin called out. His mind raced frantically. What could he say to keep them from sending Marcas straight to the gallows?

"Don't worry, Gavin. I have full faith our dear captain will treat you with the utmost respect," Marcas called back with a forced smile. His expression faltered as they pulled him roughly towards the navy ship.

"You've made a terrible mistake!" Gavin called out, this time twisting around and away from his escorts to face Hurst. He gestured at Marcas. "Release this man at once."

"I understand you're royalty, Highness, but these are Highbronian waters, and I follow the orders of *my* king," the captain said. He gestured for his men to continue leading Marcas to the other ship. "I fear so much time spent at sea with a pirate has addled your brains, Sire, if you will pardon me for saying so."

"I will not pardon you for calling me mad!" Gavin bristled, his face flushing in embarrassment and anger. "And I will not pardon you for your idiocy either! Do you really think a prince would go gallivanting about the high seas with the most notorious pirate since Dead Eye Angus Drake himself? I would ask what kind of fools you take me and my family for, but your political opinions have already been made perfectly clear. My father will hear of this! And I doubt very strongly he'll be so keen to see my sister wed to *your* king's son afterwards."

The captain's hand flew up, and the sailors yanking Marcas around halted.

"I am sorry, Your Highness, if I have caused offense. I would not wish to be the cause of any ill feelings between our monarchs." Hurst took a deep breath and eyed Gavin suspiciously. "Please. Explain yourself, then."

"That man you've just clapped in irons is a decoy," Gavin said with a calculated sigh and shake of his head. He crossed his arms over his chest. It was no great feat for him to act belaboured, since this entire ordeal had his heart pounding in his chest and his knees begging for him to sit down. If the captain didn't buy his story, they'd likely both be locked up, though for different reasons. Gavin wasn't any more interested in spending the rest of his days in an asylum than he was in seeing Marcas hanged.

"A decoy pirate? What purpose would a false Captain Drake serve?" Hurst asked, one dark brow arched in what Gavin sensed was further disbelief.

"It was my father's idea, to keep me safe while travelling incognito across the Deep. You see, what pirate in his right mind would dare challenge a man he perceived to be Captain Drake?"

Gavin continued. His shoulders slumped as his mind ran back over the events of the past few months. He glanced around the *Jewel*, glad the pirates on board seemed to be intent on keeping their ship ready to set sail once all this was over instead of piping up with the truth. "Only the plan failed to take the Crimson Queen into consideration. Captain MacLeod was too good of a decoy, and she captured us. We barely escaped with our lives."

"You had a run-in with the Crimson Queen? Where? When?" Hurst's attention flew from Gavin to Marcas and back again, his face a mask of intensity.

"She's gone," Marcas said darkly. He nodded in the direction they'd come from over the open water. "She keelhauled the *Jilted Jewel*'s captain for aiding us and called some beasts from the deep. They destroyed the *Wake*."

Hurst rolled his shoulders, the papers clasped behind his back. He nodded to the sailors holding Marcas. "Release him," he said, adjusting his hat to wipe some sweat from his brow as he turned back to Gavin. "Your Highness, please accept my sincerest apologies. I hope you'll understand my cautiousness in these terrible times. The sea is no place for honest men."

"Thank you, sir," Gavin said with a smile. "I believe you understand our caution as well." Relief washed over him as Marcas rubbed his freed wrists. He could scarcely believe he'd been successful in keeping Marcas as far from the gallows as possible. They were truly safe now, finally, and he hoped their change in luck would hold out. "It has been a very harrowing journey, more so than I ever would have guessed. Are you headed for Hroldergate by chance? The *Jilted Jewel*'s crew is only sailing as far as Blackrock."

"Yes, we are. My orders were to escort Your Highness to Hroldergate if we were able to rescue you. However, it seems you're capable of rescuing yourself," Hurst said with the first hint of a smile. He pulled the papers from behind his back and held up the wanted poster of Marcas again, comparing it to the man and shaking his head in amusement.

"I'd be dead several times over if it weren't for Captain MacLeod." Gavin shot a warm smile at Marcas as his friend went about thanking the higher-ranking members of the *Jewel*'s crew for allowing them safe passage.

"Will he be joining you, Your Highness?" Hurst asked as he gestured for his men to return to their ship.

"Yes. Marcas is my advisor and dear friend," Gavin explained. He was even more relieved when Marcas joined him near the navy captain again.

Hurst nodded in understanding and gestured for the two men to follow him across the breach. He glanced back at them once as they crossed. "It's a good thing you sent out that letter, Your Highness, or we never would have known you were in danger."

"Letter?" Gavin's brows furrowed. *What letter?* Then his eyes went wide with understanding and fear that he'd just undone every lie he'd woven together for the captain. "Oh, yes."

"That was my idea, the ransom ruse," Marcas said, flashing a bright grin at Hurst as they stepped onto the deck of the captain's ship. "Couldn't chance it falling into the wrong hands and landing us in worse trouble."

"It nearly landed you in the hangman's noose," Hurst reminded him.

"And wouldn't you place the lives of your king and his sons before your own?" Marcas countered with a tilt of his head.

"Without hesitation," Hurst said, his smile warming. He gestured at the deck of his ship and the sailors awaiting his orders. "Welcome aboard the *HMS Treadway*."

"Why the long face, Mr. MacLeod?" Gavin teased as soon as they'd retired to their cabin after a nice meal with Captain Hurst. He pressed Marcas against the door and kissed him, his lips lingering. "Where did you get that name from anyway? Is it just your usual alias?"

"It's my birth name," Marcas said. He wrapped his arms around Gavin's waist and pulled him close. Having his embrace returned didn't help his mood as much as he hoped, though, and after a few minutes Marcas pulled away. He crossed the small space and sat down on a large trunk secured to the deck, his head tilted back against the cabin wall.

It was strange, feeling like he had room to breathe after years of being on edge. The relief of suddenly being a free man, however, was heavily tinged with the mounting losses he'd experienced in the past months. His crew, his ship, his friend, and his sister were all gone. He had thirty gold coins to his name after decades of piracy. Marcas felt, for the first time, that his life had been an utter waste of time and effort.

Gavin sat next to him, silent at first, his hand sliding across Marcas's thigh to entwine their fingers.

"I won't let anything happen to you once we're in Highbron. You have my word," Gavin said, his voice soft but strong. He squeezed Marcas's hand gently.

"It wouldn't matter," Marcas said with a humourless laugh. He shook his head and closed his eyes, feeling the comforting rock of the *Treadway* as she cut through the sea. It was his sea, in part. It had been. Only he'd ruined that and everything else he'd held dear. "My best years were spent working towards thirty gold pieces. Thirty gold pieces I didn't even earn. They were a bloody gift."

"You can't berate yourself for having your livelihood snatched away from you," Gavin said, his voice firm.

"I can, since it happening at all was entirely my doing in

the end. My sodding crew never would've mutinied if I'd been half the captain my father was," Marcas insisted. He shook off Gavin's hand, stood up, and began pacing the small cabin. "And now what? Ruined by the Crimson Queen? There's a story for the fucking history books. I can't believe this!"

"Keep your voice down," Gavin chided in a cold whisper. "I'll make sure you get a reward for helping me. Enough gold for you to start over with a new ship, a new crew. If you set out straight away, you can dash any rumours that might have sprung up about your inglorious defeat. It would be like it never happened. You could say you were funded by a prince's ransom, not a king's reward. Who would dare disagree?"

"You really think that could work?" Marcas stopped in front of Gavin and ran his hands down the front of his coat, smoothing away imaginary wrinkles and dirt. He smiled again, knowing it would. Who in their right mind would dare challenge Captain Drake? Everything would work in his favour then. He'd take credit for the disappearance of the *Crimson Wake*, with Jim's memory to help him. That, along with the story of his ransoming Crakesyde's crown prince back, would guarantee him legendary status. It was perfect.

He grinned crookedly, ready to sing the praises of Gavin's intellect, but Gavin's expression stopped him from opening his mouth. Marcas's grin faded to a frown.

It wasn't perfect. It was the most dreadful idea he'd ever had.

If he couldn't have Gavin by his side, sailing across the seas with him, then it wouldn't be worth considering. They both knew well enough Gavin had royal duties to perform that didn't involve gallivanting about with a legendary pirate on purpose. Marcas couldn't ask him to willingly abandon his life or his family, and Gavin was too honour-bound a man to step away from his duties without force.

"What is it you want, Marcas? I've just promised you the things I thought you wanted most, and you look unhappy still," Gavin said, his voice thick with emotion. He cleared his throat and looked at the pair of hammocks hanging on the far wall.

"I want it all," Marcas said, feeling terribly sober. Was there no rum to be had on Hurst's ship? He'd ask the captain later, doubtful he'd get the answer he wanted. "But not if I can't have you, too."

"I'm not interested in being an afterthought." Gavin glared up at Marcas.

Suddenly the cabin felt twice as small.

"You're not an afterthought, Gavin. I just haven't had time to process all these bloody changes in my life," Marcas said, struggling to keep his voice down and his temper in check. He ran his fingers over his goatee and held up his arms in defeat. "You're all I have left. You're the only friend I have in the world. My family…as unstable as it was, they're all gone. It's difficult for *me* to deal with knowing I'm going to lose you as well once you've done your job in Highbron."

"Who said anything about losing me?" Gavin scrunched up his face as he considered Marcas's words. A flicker of understanding crossed his features. He shook his head and sighed. "You're right. I'll have to return to Crakesyde, to the castle at Auchencrow." He looked up at Marcas with a sad smile. "I'll do everything in my power to see things set to rights for you. You have my word. As your friend, not just as someone you've repeatedly saved from a terrible fate."

"I could come with you," Marcas blurted out. It was the obvious answer to their problem, and he had no idea why it hadn't struck him sooner. Likely because he was loath to give up the sea. What was he going to do on land? He knew Crakesyde's capital wasn't a coastal city.

"You're a sailor, Marcas. Would you be happy away from the sea?" The pain in Gavin's voice made Marcas's heart ache.

He wanted the answer to be yes, but he knew better. Playing courtier was what Rhona had always wanted him to do, and he hated the thought. He sat down again and rested his head in his hands, elbows braced on his thighs. "Not entirely. No."

Gavin nodded and hugged Marcas's shoulders. "We'll find a way to visit one another. To keep in touch."

Marcas leaned against him, slid an arm around Gavin's waist, and shifted him until Gavin sat astride his lap. There was no fire of lust burning between them as they held one another, only the twisting pang of knowing their time together was coming to a swift, inevitable end.

CHAPTER 21

The Highbronian castle was all hard edges and high, square ceilings with little in the way of embellishment. Everything was toned in muted browns and reds with scant white accents—a complete contrast to Castle Crakesyde's bright, golden, rounded opulence. After a brief welcome from a few key members of King Redmond's staff, Gavin and Marcas were ushered into the modest throne room with its twin wooden thrones.

"Your Highness, I present Prince Gavin of Crakesyde and his advisor, Captain MacLeod," a page announced with a sweeping bow and gesture.

Gavin and Marcas bowed, too, and Gavin opened his mouth to spout apologies for his tardiness but fell speechless when his eyes landed on a very familiar redhead seated off to the side of the throne's low dais.

"Effie?" Her name fell out of his mouth before he could catch himself, filled with shock and relief.

"Prince Gavin, a pleasure to finally meet you," King Redmond said in a rich, booming voice. He launched himself up from his throne, spry in spite of his girth and apparent age. His dark grey-streaked beard was far more majestic and full in person than in portraits Gavin had seen, and his ruddy complexion more warm. "We were pleased to receive word of your safety and arrival an hour ago. And just as shocked as we were to receive your sister last week."

"Thank you for your hospitality, Your Highness." Gavin gave a gracious nod of his head, unsure what formal words he should speak now that all he wanted to do was run to his sister, embrace her, and regale her of his adventures. She must have had a more pleasant cruise across the Deep herself, given she'd arrived ahead of him despite setting out at a later date.

King Redmond stepped down from the dais and clapped a hand on both men's shoulders. "We've been told you've faced quite the ordeal. You're both lucky to be alive, but you've helped make the seas safer with your bravery. Highbron is in your debt."

"Thank you, Your Highness," Marcas said.

Gavin glanced over at him, read the tension in his body easily, but noted his face and voice told a different story for the king. It had been nearly a month since Rhona had met her end. She'd been a dreadful person, yet she'd shown genuine affection and care for her brother and her first mate. There had been good in her, and Marcas was sure to miss that goodness for years to come.

His gaze shifted back to his own sister, who looked less excited than he felt. Their eyes met and her twitch of a smile conveyed a world of conflicting emotions. Had her hosts treated her poorly? Was Redmond the younger—the awkward-looking young man sporting a jagged scar across his cheek, standing just behind her shoulder, hand on her chair's back—a boor?

"Yes, thank you," Gavin echoed, realizing he should respond with more gracious pleasantries. It had been so long since he'd been in formal company that he felt out of place. Alone and distant in a room full of people. He longed to take Marcas's hand and feel the grounding, calloused warmth of his skin. "Although with Effie...Princess Euphemia's arrival, I'm not certain my visit has any further purpose."

"Nonsense!" King Redmond gestured to his gathered family and attendants with a wide gesture that dishevelled the ends of his beard. "You've come too far not to stay with us for a few days, a week?" He glanced over at Effie, who exchanged an odd look with him. "I don't think it should be any secret that my son and your charming sister have become quite attached to one another. I'd like to consider our alliance a surety, but we'll have to draw up the necessary papers before you depart for home."

"Oh." Gavin blinked, taken aback at the speed with which it seemed things had transpired in Effie's sphere. Yet hadn't he grown quite attached to the man beside him in a short amount of time? He put on a smile and nodded towards Prince Redmond and Effie. "Well, that's delightful news."

"Indeed," King Redmond agreed before ushering Gavin further into the room and introducing his queen, Avala, his younger son, Nolan, and finally his heir, Redmond the younger.

"Your Highness, I'd like to speak with my brother in private now," Effie said once the pleasantries had been exchanged.

"Yes, of course." King Redmond gestured towards Effie and regarded Gavin with a difficult to read expression. "Princess Euphemia has some important news to share with you."

"Follow me, Gavin." Effie stood and fluffed out her skirts. She looked as if she was restraining herself, keeping a grip on her composure with both hands.

"I'll come with you," Prince Redmond announced and started after the pair of them.

"That won't…" Effie paused. When she looked back at him, her nose went pink and her eyes became glassy. She nodded and then gestured towards Marcas. "You should bring your captain, Gavin. He'll need to hear this, too."

Something terrible had happened; that much was clear, but it had nothing to do with the Highbronian royal family if she felt comfortable with her betrothed joining them. Gavin gestured for Marcas to follow, and Effie led them into an antechamber off a hidden hallway beside the throne room.

As soon as Redmond shut the door, Effie launched herself at her brother, hugging him tightly before letting go a sobbing breath. "I thought you were dead!"

"So did I a few times. But Captain MacLeod pulled me through every scrape." Gavin clung to her and smelled the high cascade of copper ringlets piled beautifully atop her head. Flowers and a hint of fruit. A familiarity that took his heart home again, despite his being half a world away.

"You mean Captain Drake," Effie spun out of Gavin's embrace and hugged a startled Marcas. Her eyes glittered with unshed tears and mischief crept into her smile.

"Captain Drake?" Redmond spluttered. "You can't be serious!"

"Captain MacLeod." Marcas insisted, giving Effie a cursory pat on her shoulders as she released him but didn't stop staring at his face.

"I spent years dreaming about running away to join your crew. I stared at portraits and sketches of you in every book on piracy I could get my hands on. You can't fool me." Effie let out a nervous laugh and dabbed at her eyes with a handkerchief pulled from inside her sleeve.

"If he's a pirate—" Redmond stood up straight, hand straying to his hip for a sword that wasn't there. The prince glowered, frowned, looked between the three of them. His gaze settled on Effie, and his expression softened. "Father can't know."

"I can't be a pirate without a ship or a crew," Marcas grumbled.

"Marcas..." Gavin touched his shoulder without thinking of how it might look.

"I want you two to tell me everything that's happened to you," Effie said, taking a seat on the settee and gesturing for the men to sit as well. Redmond sat beside her and took her hand in both of his. "But first I have to tell you what's happened in Crakesyde. The reason for my journey."

"Yes, of course." Gavin sat in the chair across from her, perched on the edge of the dark, cushioned leather.

Marcas sat more carefully in the chair beside him, leather squeaking in protest as he settled back against it. He didn't look as comfortable as he had at sea, his carefree rakish poise gone.

Effie took a deep breath and wadded her handkerchief in her fist. She licked her lips. Redmond squeezed her hand and murmured something into her ear.

"Father's become...more unstable. He's angry all the time, about everything, at everyone, but he won't take proper care of himself, let alone his duties. After they discovered the way he'd sent you off... The King's Council has elected a regent," she said, retaining her composure with a press of her lips.

"What?" A glut of conflicting emotions ran through Gavin at once. Disbelief, hope, sadness, and the heavy weights of fear and insecurity fought for dominance. This was what Crakesyde desperately needed if it was going to retain its island colonies in the Deep. Countless resources and strategic ports would be lost to pirates, independence, or other nations if their navy remained bound to their mainland shores. Not to mention the human lives lost to pirates with no interest in the value of a life not their own. But to have his worst fears about his father's behaviour in the past few years confirmed… Senility had set in and robbed him of the man he'd admired and loved with an open heart in childhood.

"King Malcolm?" Marcas leaned forward in his seat, the groan of leather adding to the awkward silence that fell over the room.

Effie nodded.

"If he still held any authority, he never would have let you travel here without word from me," Gavin said softly. Even if Gavin had been presumed dead at some point, their father would have sent another diplomat to Highbron first, he felt sure. Or perhaps he'd do nothing, now.

"The royal doctor, Doctor Tannet, says it's a consequence of old age." Effie looked down at where her hand sat encased in Redmond's, his light-brown fingers laced with her ivory ones. "I came to tell you in person. To send you back home on the ship I sailed in on."

"If father's lost the will to rule and you're here…who's sitting on the throne?" Gavin's mind raced, thinking of the terrible things that could be happening in Castle Crakesyde at that very moment. He needed to leave as soon as possible. The risk of offending King Redmond and his family would have to be taken. His kingdom, his people, didn't deserve to be subjected to some power-hungry usurper who might see an ailing king's absence as a welcome to the crown. The likely candidate sprang to mind. "Uncle Albarn?"

"Uncle Albarn tried to argue blood rights, but the King's Council denied him based on his constant drunkenness and poor public favour. Duke Waldren is sitting as regent until your return or six months pass with no word from you," Effie said. She smirked. "Now's your chance to escape the crown, Gav."

For a moment, Gavin pictured himself and Marcas sailing back to their little island with supplies. They could feign death to the world and hide away, together, into old age. A home for just the two of them. A small garden. The lush jungle their private sanctuary. It was a beautiful vision, but it would be tainted with the painful knowledge of Gavin's wilful refusal to rise to the challenges of sovereignty.

He'd survived this far in the face of violence, madness, and pirate politics, which were worse than cutthroat. He could lean on his Council to help him until he found his bearings as king. His first order of business would be to send some of the naval fleet out to the colonies to protect them and set them to rights. Piracy couldn't continue its foothold, but Gavin hated the idea of the sweeping anti-pirate stance Highbron held. Pirates were men and women trying to make something for themselves. Some of them were violent at heart, but many just wanted to survive. To be comfortable. To enjoy the sea life and find a smattering of happiness. No, he'd much rather go the route Naavet and Anthea had taken with privateers. Commissions would be paid and provisions supplied, allowing them to escort merchant ships and help protect the island colonies under royal protection. He'd make honest sailors of those pirates who wanted more than violence and excess. And Marcas would be...

"No, I won't run from it." Gavin turned to Marcas, brows furrowed. His idea wouldn't solve their problem entirely, but it felt right. So long as Marcas agreed. "How would you feel about privateering for Crakesyde? Under the name Captain Drake."

"I'd... Privateering?" Marcas canted his head back, brows drawn, and let out a bark of a laugh. "Piracy in the name of the crown—*your* crown? I'd be a fool to say no."

"My father won't take kindly to finding he's been lied to," Prince Redmond said, his tone dour.

"That's an excellent point. I shouldn't like to offend him in the first place, however our circumstances are—" He glanced at Marcas again. "It's lies or the gallows."

"If you tell him just that, he'll understand. He's a practical man, but a romantic at heart. He wouldn't have forced me to marry Effie if we'd hated one another, even though he desired a marital alliance with Crakesyde." Redmond looked thoughtful for a moment. "If you pen a letter explaining everything before you leave, I'll give it to him several days after you've left. That way, he won't feel the added insult of hearing about it second-hand, months from now."

"Perfect, thank you." Gavin was more and more impressed with Prince Redmond, and while Gavin was the elder prince by several years, he felt he could learn from Redmond by example. It was a shame he needed to cut their visit short. "We'll return to Crakesyde tomorrow afternoon. I—"

"But you've only just arrived," Effie protested. "You haven't even really met Redmond yet."

Her life had been turned upside down while he'd been away, and now she likely felt he was abandoning her for something he'd never wanted. However, she was intelligent and strong; she had to be able to put her own feelings aside.

"You know I have to put the needs of the kingdom before my own needs. I'd stay here a month, but it wouldn't be enough time, would it?" Gavin fixed his eyes on his sister, imploring her to understand.

"Never. But that doesn't make this any easier." She wiped at her nose with her handkerchief.

"We'll visit. During the winter months," Redmond offered with a warm smile. "Effie's been telling me about your milder winters and the seasonal festivities you all share to spread warmth and cheer during the cold months. Here the winter storms often make it impossible to travel for days, let alone go ice skating or sleigh racing."

"That sounds lovely," Effie said with a nod, smiling again as she leaned against him. "Do you see how he's charmed me?"

"Yes," Gavin said, his own smile returning with warmth that filled his chest. It was a true relief to know his sister would be happy in Highbron, and with a man who clearly cared for her.

"Now," Marcas clapped his hands together and settled back in his chair as if he owned it, a smirk on his handsome face. "Let me tell you the story of how Captain Drake charmed a prince."

"Kidnapped," Gavin said, fighting a smile. "The word you're searching for is 'kidnapped'."

"I knew it!" Effie grinned and pointed at Gavin. "I could see it in your eyes. You've fallen in love!"

That wasn't something he was entirely comfortable admitting in such certain terms. His face burned with mild embarrassment, but he knew there was no judgement from her. Only joy.

"So it's true what they say about you?" Redmond asked, looking at Marcas with his dark brows arched high. "That you've no interest in women?"

Marcas let out a slow sigh. "Yes, Your Highness."

"Would you two mind…before you leave…could you speak with my brother, Nolan? There are no laws against homosexuality in Highbron, but he finds himself under pressure from our parents to marry a suitable woman." Redmond cleared his throat. "He's only fourteen, but now that I'm betrothed…"

"Do your parents know?" Gavin asked.

"No, he's too afraid they'll be disappointed in him," Redmond said with a sigh.

"We'll see what we can do to help," Marcas said, his smile earnest.

"Thank you." Redmond nodded and then grinned when Effie leaned up to kiss his cheek.

"All right, story time," Effie said, bouncing a little on the settee. She snuggled against Redmond's side, and he slipped an arm around her waist.

"It all started with the *Ebon Drake*'s capture of the merchant ship *Maiden Fair*," Marcas began.

CHAPTER 22

Sleep didn't absolve Marcas of his doubts in agreeing to Gavin's privateering solution. Neither did their pleasant breakfast with the royal family, where they made it a point to display subtle but clear signs of their more than platonic affection for one another.

"Will there be a Crakesydian royal wedding in the near future?" Queen Avala asked in her lilting Naavetian accent as the dishes were cleared away by serving staff. She gestured between Gavin and Marcas with her half-empty teacup before taking a sip.

Gavin cleared his throat and turned a delightful shade of scarlet. Effie giggled into her hand.

"Prince Gavin isn't yet betrothed," Marcas said and drank down the last of his cold tea. He wanted more of the full-bodied brandy King Redmond had shared with him the evening before, but the Highbronians didn't look to be morning drinkers. It was probably for the best, or he might have burst out laughing at the queen's question.

"Oh? But I thought... Pardon me, then." Queen Avala shrugged.

"I don't think it's something I can…rush into." Gavin spared a glance across the table at Prince Nolan, who looked as if he wanted to crawl under his chair.

"It's never too soon to start producing heirs," King Redmond said without looking up from the papers spread out before him at the end of the table.

"Dear, I was speaking about Prince Gavin and Mr. MacLeod." Avala pressed her light-brown hand to her forehead.

"Oh, right, well then, you'll want a consort for heirs." Redmond waved his hand towards Gavin, still buried in reading over his documents. "That's how they handle things in Naavet. Clever, really."

"I hadn't thought about that possibility," Gavin said, sitting up straighter while the tension left his face. He smiled at Marcas and took his hand.

"Don't ask me to marry you at the breakfast table." Marcas laughed, covering his nerves. How could he say no? But how could he say yes? They'd hardly see one another if he headed Gavin's privateering operation. Or, if he changed his mind, he'd hardly see the open waters of the Deep while tucked away inside a stuffy castle in the centre of the world's largest landmass. He wasn't sure he could live without either of them for very long.

"You have to be romantic about it, Gav," Effie said and shot a smile at Nolan, who smiled back. "It's a love match, after all."

"I'm sure I'll think of something suitable," Gavin said with a nod.

THE WINDS WERE favourable and strong, whipping Gavin's hair out of its low ponytail. The northern weather had already turned far cooler than he'd experienced on his journey across the Deep. Effie clung to him while the crew of the HMS *Eudora*—named after their late mother—loaded the last of their supplies.

"Promise you'll write," she said for the third time, tugging on the handsome emerald cloak King Redmond had gifted him. She sniffled and ducked her head against a fresh gust of cold wind. "Twice. Copy every letter and send them on different ships in case something happens."

"You'll know exactly what's happening back home, I promise." Gavin chuckled and held on to her, already anticipating return correspondence about her life in Highbron. When she took a step back, he couldn't believe how mature she looked. The sea changed people, he thought with reverence.

"Here, Effie." Prince Redmond stepped up beside her and lifted the fur-trimmed hood of her cloak up over her windswept hair.

"Take good care of my future brother-in-law," Gavin said as she finally released him to turn into her fiancé's embrace. It was obvious to him why it had taken such a short time for the two of them to fall for one another. They were well matched, and he was more than grateful for it. Redmond the younger seemed to have a good head for diplomacy, too, which would serve him well politically as well as romantically.

"Only if you take good care of mine." Effie's bright smile was delightfully infectious.

Farewells were exchanged, and soon Gavin and Marcas stood on the main deck of the *Eudora*, pressed against one another as they waved goodbye to the diminishing figures on the docks. Effie and her new family became indistinguishable from the rocky red outcroppings that jutted up behind Hroldergate's shipyard.

Gavin peered up at the green Crakesydian flag snapping back and forth in the high winds. He'd thought so many times he'd never again see the familiar black crow, its golden crown hovering above its head, beak open and ready to sip from the golden goblet raised in its claw. He leaned against Marcas and then turned his face to look at him. "I accomplished my mission. Thanks to you, I get to return home in one piece."

Not everyone had been so lucky. It staggered him to think of all the lives lost along their journey. His chest ached with the understanding that he and Marcas had become inexplicably tied to one another. Would he be able to stand being apart from Marcas for months at a time?

"And thanks to you, I'll have someplace new to call home," Marcas's smile didn't quite reach his eyes, but Gavin reasoned it could be the fault of the wind.

"I want you to be happy, no matter what it means," Gavin said. Marcas had experienced too much loss, and all at once. Gavin couldn't imagine losing both his sister and his home, the security of his place in the world. He couldn't imagine losing Marcas, either, but taking him away from the sea for selfish reasons would be reprehensible.

"It means being with you, sharing our lives *together*," Marcas said and kissed beside Gavin's ear, holding on to him tighter as they gazed out over the polished rail at the grey-blue sea. "But it'll also mean sailing…being apart for intolerable stretches of time."

"If only our capital wasn't landlocked," Gavin mused aloud. It would make things easier to have his primary residence a port town. They could go sailing for pleasure once his privateering enterprise was well under way, and Marcas might be interested in hanging up his captain's coat. "I could convince you to retire and sail me around Auchen Bay."

Marcas made a strained noise in his throat. "Gavin…once

you're coronated, couldn't you move the capital to Crowsmouth?"

"I suppose I could." Gavin's brows furrowed as his mind raced through everything that would involve. It wouldn't be a mere change of residence; it would mean a change in location for all royal business. Decrees would have to be made and distributed across the countryside and out to the colonies. Letters would have to be sent to their allies. The estate at Crowsmouth, Wardwell House, was certainly large enough to accommodate the needs of the royal family and serving staff. Situated atop the bluff overlooking Auchen Bay, it was an older, beautiful set of buildings done in a less grandiose style than the castle at Auchencrow. The stables and carriage house would need updating, and the gardens, which had been left to grow wild for several years. "I'm not sure my father would want to leave the castle, though. It's been years since he's left without being coerced by his Council. If it's been senility encroaching all this time, I can't imagine he'd willingly move house. Let alone with me having 'usurped' his crown."

"Would he need to go with you?"

Brows furrowed, Gavin considered the pros and cons of being separated from his ailing father long term. King Malcolm's continued excellent care was a given. Wouldn't it be best to let the man remain where he'd be comfortable if he so chose? Being free from the daily verbal abuses levelled at Gavin for so many years had been a relief in its own way, though he'd scarcely noticed its absence in the face of so much adventure. In the quieter setting of home, he'd feel the full brunt again. It wasn't appealing.

"I suppose not. We'd both be happier apart, I think, but I'll leave it up to him, of course," Gavin said, taking a deep breath of cold sea air. It chilled his lungs in a way that made him feel keenly alive, comfortably wrapped in his cloak and Marcas's half embrace. He smiled at Marcas and kissed his lightly stubbled jaw. "He's going to hate you."

Marcas laughed, a deep sound that grew into a thin sigh. He turned Gavin in his arms and cupped his jaw, brushing the rough pad of his thumb over Gavin's cheek. "And what else would I expect a father to think of the thieving rogue who's seduced his son?"

"Your Highness," a strong, feminine voice said, pulling his attention from Marcas's brilliant green eyes.

"Yes, Commander Mulrayne?" Gavin smiled at the stout, solidly built brunette. Her stern blue eyes and cool fair complexion reminded him of portraits of his paternal grandmother. He'd have to promote her to captain once the journey home had concluded—a reward for safeguarding his sister, and now himself and Marcas, across the Deep.

"It looks as if the storm may catch us yet, Highness. I recommend both of you retire to your cabin below decks. I'll be happy to escort you." She bowed her tricorn-covered head, the green-and-gold ribbon rosette attached to the hat fluttering as wildly as the strands of hair escaping the thick braid down her back.

"Yes, of course. You mentioned, before we set sail, it's the same cabin my sister occupied on your voyage to Highbron," Gavin said as they followed the commander towards the stairs.

"Indeed. She remained quite comfortable for the duration," Commander Mulrayne said. She led them to the cabin in question, which was modestly sized and furnished with a high-sided bed, their travelling trunk, a desk with chair, and a chaise upholstered with white-and-gold brocade.

"I doubt she spent much time in here," Gavin commented more to himself than the commander.

"Only when pressed, Highness," she said with a chuckle. "Princess Euphemia was a delight to have on board. We'll all miss her spirited presence."

CHAPTER 23

T HE *E UDORA* LISTED HARD, SENDING THE DESK CHAIR SKIMMING back until the feet caught the edge of the narrow rug running the length of the room. Gavin dug his fingers into the rolled arm of the chaise, book forgotten. He still slid into Marcas, who leaned hard against Gavin to keep from tumbling off the cushioned bench.

"Don't stop now, we've just got to the swashbuckling," Marcas said with a laugh. He stretched an arm around Gavin, sandwiching his prince against the chaise's high side, and gripped the backrest to keep them both seated while the ship rocked.

He hadn't been read to since Rhona had abandoned fairy tales in favour of fencing. It was something he hadn't realised he'd missed. Though he was perfectly capable of reading for himself, he didn't much enjoy it. Listening to Gavin's voice, his stately inflection and gentle swells of emotion as he read about the pirate hero stealing from wealthy rivals to give to poor settlers, took him to a warmer, simpler time. When his sister had been more filled with awe and an adventurous heart than the desire to fill the seas with blood. When his new father had shown him what parental care looked and felt like, easily replacing the couple who'd brought him into the world.

"Can't get enough, can you?" Gavin grinned and shook his head. As he opened the book again, a thrice-folded piece of paper fell into his lap.

"What's this?" Marcas plucked the paper up and flicked it open as the ship rocked again, making them cling to the chaise once more. The chair toppled over on the rug, but they paid it no mind; the rest of the furniture in the cabin was secured to the deck. "Dearest Gav—"

"Effie must have left the book for me," Gavin said, his smile brightening. "I'm not surprised."

"*Dearest Gav,*" Marcas continued from the beginning. "*When I read this book I thought of you, so I'm leaving it tucked in the desk in hopes you'll find it. I think you'll love the main character's adventure. The author is Anthean like mother, and they banned his book in Anthea for being too scandalous. I hope you're safe and Prince Redmond isn't a complete prat. With love, Effie. P.S. I still can't decide if I hope you had amazing adventures on your way to Highbron or no adventures at all. I told the Council about your strange trip, and well, hopefully you know the rest by now.*"

"She only acquired it because it was banned somewhere." Gavin shot Marcas a humoured look before lifting the book to find his place again. "Too much promoting of piracy in these pages."

"Anthea's not so harsh against pirates, though. It's more of a testament to the success of privateering, so I don't understand why they'd find it bothersome," Marcas said with a shrug of one shoulder. He tucked the letter into the breast pocket on Gavin's coat in case he wanted to keep it.

"Hm, true." Gavin pressed against Marcas as the ship rode the waves hard. He looked over at him—his flush apparent even in the unsteady lantern light—cleared his throat, and picked the story up where he left off. *"His cutlass dropped to the dock with a steely clatter. 'Avast, knave!' I said, holding my blade to Pete's neck in fresh threat to his life. 'Surrender, or else face your fate.' Eyes wide with something more than fear, he raised his hands freely and said, 'I've already surrendered, Aleksar! Can't you see you've stolen more than my captain's gold! You've stolen my…'"*

"My what?" Marcas pressed, unsure why Gavin had stopped again.

"My *heart*." Gavin blinked at the book, skimmed ahead, turned the page. He sucked in a sharp breath. "Oh…well. Yes. We hadn't quite reached the scandal yet."

Marcas swallowed and wetted his lips.

He didn't have to know what the printed pages contained to become aroused at the thoughts Gavin's reaction inspired. Their first sexual encounter had been under duress, and half under false pretences. The harried journey afterward had left him aching for more than the closeness of sleeping side by side and the soft familiarity of Gavin's lips. How one man could effect such a change in him, he'd never know. The mystery of that attraction—one that encompassed so much more than lust—wasn't something he felt driven to unravel. It was something to sink into, something to lose himself in and know that, even without it being expressed in words, he wouldn't be truly lost with Gavin there beside him.

His lips brushed against Gavin's ear, and he spoke softly over the roar of rain and waves outside their sanctuary. "It's high time we indulged in a little scandal of our own, don't you think?"

Gavin stuck Effie's note between the pages and slapped the book shut. "I don't know how it's done." He tilted his head to the side and slid his hand across Marcas's thigh to the prominent bulge demanding attention. "Show me?"

"There're so many ways." Marcas kissed the soft, lightly tanned stretch of Gavin's long neck, inching his way back up to his earlobe with lips, tongue, and a nip of his teeth. The tiny grunt from his lover was all the encouragement he needed. "I'll show you my favourite."

Marcas captured Gavin's earlobe in his teeth and then flicked his tongue at the captive flesh. The gasp and blind grope of his erection made him smirk. He hadn't lost his touch after all.

He guided Gavin carefully to his feet, book abandoned on the chaise, and they kissed as they fumbled to undress one another and retain their balance. Thunder cracked and they jerked apart, only to laugh at their unnecessary fright.

Gavin splayed his hands over the dark hair covering Marcas's chest and trailed his fingers over the contours of his chest, pausing to squeeze his dark nipples between his fingers before unfastening Marcas's belt. His gentle explorations continued while Marcas took his turn to unfasten Gavin's breeches and shove them down his hips and leanly muscled thighs. Eager to touch, he brushed his fingers over the nest of tight russet curls surrounding Gavin's hard, reddened cock.

On their island, he hadn't been able to see his lover clearly as they'd drunkenly pleasured one another in the dark. In the privacy of their cabin, however, Marcas let his gaze wander as freely as his hands, taking in the thickness of Gavin's shaft and the sensual weight of his balls.

The ship listed again, and they fell back against the high side of the bed together, protectively holding one another with half their clothes around their knees and the rest discarded on the rug.

"Best we lie down, love," Marcas murmured.

With a few quick movements, they finished disrobing. Gavin climbed onto the bed while Marcas opened the trunk and rummaged around for a leather-encased bottle of sweet oil. He kept the highest quality, made from Anthean olives, and it happened to be an excellent lubricant for more than his pistols. Luckily, acquiring a fresh bottle before departing from Highbron hadn't proved difficult.

Trunk secured, Marcas stumbled to the bed, his hand slamming against the wall to brace himself. He wasn't about to let a storm stop him from feeling Gavin's body flush against him, nothing between them but friction and heat. His eyes raked over Gavin's lean frame. The masculine beauty of his slender build, the gracefulness of his limbs, and the sultry look in his eyes as he stroked himself had Marcas at full hardness again. He tucked the bottle into the bedcovers where they bunched against the high side of the bed and bent down over Gavin.

He steadied himself against the bed with both hands and dipped his head down to taste Gavin's cockhead before it disappeared inside his foreskin again. Gavin gasped and stayed his hand, shaking with need or cold—Marcas couldn't be sure. He glanced up to ensure he wasn't doing anything out of line.

"Don't stop," Gavin whispered.

"Keep stroking for me. And try not to come." Marcas kissed and licked at Gavin's prick, eyes slipping closed as he focused on the lightly salty taste of skin and the breathy sounds Gavin made. His tongue darted beneath Gavin's foreskin before his mouth followed Gavin's hand down over the thick shaft.

Gavin moaned in quick, staccato bursts as Marcas bobbed over him in a messy rhythm. When Gavin's hand became as erratic as his breathing, Marcas pulled away and stretched his arms.

"*Please.*" Gavin reached up for him, but Marcas shook his head.

"Roll over."

Gavin was quick to comply and brushed the loose waves of his hair out of his face, looking debauched, expectant, and nervous as Marcas freed the cork from the bottle. He drizzled the oil on his cock and stroked it, making sure to coat it well. Then, for good measure, he poured some between Gavin's round cheeks and down his thighs.

"I've heard of one way men have sex," Gavin murmured, shaking again with the obvious tension in his body. Everything Marcas had done to relax him had been undone. "It seems…painful."

"If done poorly, yes. But we won't do that tonight, love. It's not the best choice for a long journey at sea. Just relax." Marcas recorked the bottle and set it aside, shifting to straddle Gavin's thighs and smooth his oiled hands up and down the pink scars marring his back. He shoved away the unpleasant memories of how Gavin had become marked, knowing the striations would fade with time, and focused instead on easing the tension back out of the man's shoulders. As a more gentle roll of thunder grumbled outside, he worked his hands down to massage Gavin's arse, spreading his cheeks and sliding his thumbs between them.

"*Oh,*" Gavin uttered into the pillow and arched his hips up off the bed.

Marcas teased his entrance with alternating swipes of his thumbs until Gavin began to hump the bed, arms tucked up under the pillow. That was the mindless abandon of a wanton, pleasured man, and Marcas was ready to join his lover in courting that emotion. Quickly he refreshed the oil and settled over Gavin, forearms pressed tight against his sides, and slid the heat of his cock between the cool smoothness of Gavin's arse cheeks. Marcas matched each thrust against his lover with a kiss to his shoulders. It didn't take long for Gavin to buck and rock beneath him, meeting his body as best he could while under his weight, rutting against the bed as much as Marcas rutted against him, moaning his enjoyment.

Gavin's breath hitched, and he stilled, his body relaxing beneath Marcas, but Marcas hadn't finished yet. He shifted onto his side in the narrow bed and pulled Gavin close to him, back to chest. Gavin had become languid and pliable after his release, which made it easy for Marcas to guide his still aching hardness between his lover's oiled thighs.

As he thrust into the tighter space, Gavin reached back to hold his waist and slid his arm under Marcas's, touch sensual and firm. They tilted their faces to one another's, necks craned to meet in a hungry kiss. Marcas bucked wildly, lips and tongue dancing with Gavin's. It was something he'd never done before while having sex, never thought to do in the heat of the moment. With Gavin it felt right. *Necessary.* What other act could so perfectly express their affection and desire for one another? He grunted and groaned into Gavin's mouth as he came. Settling his shoulder back against the cabin wall, he pulled Gavin against him.

Unmindful of the mess they'd made, Gavin shifted to face Marcas. He ran his fingers through Marcas's chest hair, seemingly fascinated. "That was brilliant," he said softly, looking up with sleepy, sated eyes. "I hope you brought enough oil for the duration."

"We might have to procure some more before we reach Crakesyde," Marcas admitted with a humoured huff. He kissed Gavin's damp forehead and pulled the edge of the blanket up over him. If he'd created a monster, he certainly wouldn't complain. There'd be no better way to spend their time in close quarters.

"Good." Gavin sighed and settled into Marcas's arms. "Next time, can I make love to you?"

Marcas's chest ached with tight warmth. Of course Gavin could put proper words to what they'd just done. "As many times as you'd like."

CHAPTER 24

WALKING UP THE WHITE-AND-BLACK MARBLE STEPS OF CASTLE Crakesyde with a crown on his head made Gavin feel at once important and insignificant. The cheering throng had followed his and Marcas's slow carriage ride from the coronation at Auchencrow's Council Hall with great fanfare.

Somehow, knowing so many Crakesydians shared the same relief he and the Council did over his ascension to the throne made him feel less like a fraud. It would take time to acclimate, he'd been told by his aides. Even Duke Waldren, who'd been ready to resume his place on the King's Council, had shared words of encouragement and patience. There was still a spark of attraction for the man, but having wed Marcas as soon as they'd arrived in Crowsmouth the week before put his mildly lustful thoughts in perspective. No flights of mental fancy would ever compare to the depths of his bond with his husband. A husband he wouldn't have taken so soon if it weren't for the rising tide of questions and rumours surrounding the former Captain Drake's change from villain to national hero.

One final turn and wave at the crowd and they were done with being a spectacle for the day.

"Welcome home, for now, my prince," Gavin said as they entered the castle through its grand front doors, unable to keep the grin off his face at Marcas's look of indignation.

"Remind me again how long you'll be doing that before you get bored of it?" Marcas adjusted his simple emerald-studded coronet, one brow arched at Gavin.

"But you're actually a prince now." Gavin laughed and pulled Marcas into an embrace, appreciating the way he looked in the smart white-and-gold dress uniform of the Crakesydian navy. The green cape with gold details, slung over one shoulder, was the perfect addition to his formal ensemble.

A smirk overtook Marcas's face. "Rhona'd love this. All of it."

"What about you? Still think you'll be content enough to go from infamous pirate captain to prince of Crakesyde and admiral of His Majesty's privateer fleet?" Gavin fussed with Marcas's rank insignia and the golden cords looping down over the front of his double-breasted coat. A small part of him worried Marcas would find his new roles too inhibiting. Husband. Prince. Admiral. All three tethered him to different things.

"My father never would have done it." He let out a huff of a laugh. "The countryside's already eating it up. It won't be long before the historians are knocking down our door. It's a bloody good tale, from pirate to prince. Bet it spreads like wildfire abroad."

The sheer delight in Marcas's face was more than enough to smother Gavin's doubts about his happiness. He hated to ruin the moment of joy with the post-coronation duty they needed to face, but once he allowed the weight of that duty to occupy the forefront of his mind, Gavin's smile faltered, and he sobered with a nod.

"It's time to introduce you to my father."

"Everything will be fine. I promise." Marcas yanked his gloves off, tucked them into the pocket of his breeches and then plucked off Gavin's gloves one finger at a time. He took both of Gavin's hands and stepped in to place a warm kiss on his lips. "And if it isn't, we'll leave him be and try again another day."

"Duke Waldren's kept him abreast of current events, at least. So you— *We* won't come as a surprise," Gavin said as he led the way through the brightly sunlit halls with their gaudy golden decor and clusters of paintings of all sizes. Ornately framed family portraits began to outnumber pastoral landscapes and depictions of historical figures the deeper into the spiralling halls they travelled.

Serving staff greeted them in passing, some pausing to express happiness at Gavin's return, marriage, and coronation. Seeing familiar faces and exchanging pleasantries further buoyed Gavin's spirits, though his racing heart hadn't got the message. There'd be a more formal introduction of Marcas to the entire staff in the coming days, but that wasn't as immediate a concern as visiting his father.

Two guards in full armour bearing the royal insignia stood outside the arched door to the former king's chambers, swords at their hips, glaives in hand. The beautifully embellished polearms were more than decorative.

"Is my father amenable to visitors today?" Gavin asked, unsure of the proper way to speak to the guards in such a situation. He'd witnessed his father bark orders and demand things of the castle's staff in dramatically formal language for years. That wouldn't be his tack. The serving staff weren't paid to deal with verbal abuse.

"He's never amenable to visitors, Your Highness," the

guard on the left said, her brows furrowed beneath the lifted visor of her helmet.

"I see." Gavin sighed, his good mood evaporating, and turned to Marcas. "Perhaps I should talk to him alone first."

"I think that's a terrible idea," Marcas said. He took Gavin's hand and squeezed it, adding his strength and resolve to Gavin's before it could retreat. "We're in this together, and I'll stand beside you when my duties don't take me elsewhere. Speaking to your father. Protecting the realm. Life. I didn't join hands with you in front of the people of Crowsmouth to turn around days later and let you go it alone with your old man."

A shout came from the somewhere beyond the closed door, and a moment later, it opened. Doctor Tannet, dressed in her doctor's garb of a tunic and trousers, smiled at Gavin and Marcas and then opened the door wider before bowing and ushering them in.

"Come in, please. It's good to see you, Highness. My *king*. And my prince. What a delightful series of events!" she said, speaking softly.

Gavin's instinct was to reject the title, but no, it was his now. He nodded to the doctor as they entered his father's private sitting room, and she closed the door behind them. Her thick mane of black curls was pulled back from her dark face with a fringed length of green-and-gold cloth. She looked as if she'd aged ten years in the span of a few months, the lines around her eyes no doubt caused by having to frequently attend a man whose decency had been robbed from him by the cruelties of time.

"How is he faring?" Gavin asked, matching her hushed tone.

"He's…stable for now, but he struggles to find the desire to care for much of anything besides quiet," Doctor Tannet said and put a hand on Gavin's shoulder, just like Doctor

Milston had done when his mother had died of the wasting fever. "Make sure you both keep your voices down, please, just like we're doing now. It will…smooth things along."

"Duke Waldren informed me that he's become bedridden for the last month and a half. He sleeps much of the time and doesn't care to speak to anyone but you." Gavin glanced up at the open doorway to the bedchamber, silence and candlelight emanating from within. For a moment, his father's chambers felt as foreboding as a tomb.

"Yes. He likes to talk, but he's no longer willing or able to listen. He's not as prone to shouting outbursts as he had been for the past few years, but I'm afraid it's more due to apathy than a lack of—" She took a deep breath and exhaled. "—strong opinions." She squeezed Gavin's shoulder in kindly support. "Are you ready?"

"Not at all," Gavin said, a sad smile twisting his lips into a grimace. He took Marcas's hand again and walked into his father's bedchamber anyway, knowing that he'd never be ready.

Malcolm lay propped up on a collection of pillows in his large, four-poster bed. The sheer inner curtains were drawn across the foot of the bed, hiding any details.

"Is that you, boy?"

Gavin swallowed past the lump in his throat and, at a subtle nudge from Marcas, moved around the side of the bed with Marcas at his side. His father looked like he'd put on a little weight, but something about the set of his narrow jaw and the faraway look in his eyes struck Gavin as *off*.

"Hello, father. This is Marcas…Marcas Drake. My husband. Marcas, my father, Malcolm."

"It's good to finally meet you, sir," Marcas said with a bow, but he didn't let go of Gavin's hand.

Malcolm grunted and shifted against his pillows,

squinting at Gavin and then Marcas. "You don't look like a pirate."

"That's good, given I've retired." Marcas shook a little as he fought a laugh, lips pressed together in a smile that calmed Gavin's nerves.

"I don't know who you are, but you're not Captain Drake. A farmer. Some drifter sailor or—" Malcolm flapped his hand in the air. "—that blasted foppish traitor Dunmire's wife's fourth bastard cousin from Hesleden. Whoever you are, they tell me you're my son-in-law."

"Yes, sir, I am." Marcas's expression turned stony.

Gavin braced himself for the worst, but his father made a dismissive noise and stared off towards the heavy curtains drawn across the far side of the bed, hands folded over his stomach.

"Father, I trust Duke Waldr—"

"Dunmire," Malcolm insisted, firm yet oddly calm.

Gavin wished Doctor Tannet had warned him about his father taking the duke for his enemy, but he should have guessed it would happen. He found he was shamefully grateful his father's enmity hadn't been turned towards him for replacing him on the throne. In fact, he found it the most odd that the man hadn't yet said anything cruel about him or his ascension to the throne.

"I trust he told you I was successful in my endeavour in Highbron," Gavin said, forcing himself to speak softly despite the inclination to be more forceful with his voice.

"Yes. Effie has married Redmond the younger by now," Malcolm stated as though discussing the weather.

"Aren't you pleased, father?"

Malcolm didn't respond but didn't gaze off at the bed curtains again. Uncomfortable silence filled the room, and Gavin became self-conscious of his own breathing, the weight of the crown on his head, and the stifling nature of his cravat. Gavin returned the firm squeeze Marcas gave his hand and realised he was sweating, not only from the warmth in the enclosed room, but because of his heightened nerves. He let go of Marcas's hand to wipe his palm on the side of his breeches while his father looked at him, yet through him.

"Father," he said at a normal volume.

"Quiet!" Malcolm hissed.

"Father," he began again, low and gentle. "Aren't you pleased about Effie's marriage and the alliance with Highbron?"

"Doctor Tannet says I should be." Malcolm scratched the grey stubble on his jaw and the side of his neck where his thin white hair fell over his shoulder.

"It's what you wanted," Gavin said.

Malcolm shrugged. "What I want is *quiet*. Yet you keep blathering on. Don't you have a kingdom to run, King Gavin the fourth? Or are you Dunmire's puppet, leaving you all the time in the world to bother a tired old man?"

Gavin's mouth fell open, but he was at a loss for anything more to say. He never could have guessed that his father not caring would be so much worse than him caring too much.

"We'll leave you to rest, sir," Marcas said and took Gavin by the elbow.

"Trust the spy to have sense," Malcolm muttered and shifted onto his side, turning his back to them.

Gavin hesitated. There was so much he'd wanted to tell his father, so much he'd expected him to be angry about, to *care* about with the deep anger that had consumed him for years. He'd already become a different man than he'd been in Gavin's childhood. Gavin saw he'd been wrong to blame his mother's death for his father's personality shift. It hadn't been trauma at all, but early senility creeping up on him all the while. Malcolm had taken a wife in his late forties, insisting on a political marriage to build needed ties with Anthea, and he was nearing seventy now.

Would it be right to leave him alone, even though it was what he said he wanted? Gavin didn't have any answers. He wasn't sure anyone else would, either.

"Father, I've decided to move the capital to Crowsmouth to better oversee our naval and sea trade operations. I'll institute a fleet of privateers that Marcas will head, and we'll be living at Wardwell House. Would you like to come with us?" Gavin blurted out in a rush.

Malcolm scrunched his shoulders and rolled onto his back again, dragging the covers around with him. "It's your kingdom; do what you like." He tugged at the edge of the covers in an attempt to untangle them. "Doctor! I need my rest!"

Gavin winced at the shouts but regained what composure he had left and nodded at his father. "Good day, father."

"Good day, sir," Marcas said.

They apologised to Doctor Tannet on their way out, but Gavin wouldn't let her dismissal of his apology sink in.

All the way through the castle he showed Marcas different rooms, different statues and paintings, and introduced him to serving staff members he knew. Yet his mind was tangled up with a painful mix of grief and guilt.

Finally, they reached his private chambers, which looked exactly as he'd left them. Someone had been good enough to dust and sweep during his absence, he noted as he sat down at his desk.

"A sitting room, a miniature library, a bedchamber, your own privy... And I thought Rhona's cabin on the *Crimson Wake* was extravagant," Marcas said as he threw open the curtains on the picture windows to let the late afternoon sunlight in. He peered down over the castle's rear gardens with their towering willows and central hedge maze. "What's beyond the far wall? It looks like nothing, not even a windmill or silo."

"Dun's Mire. A great bog." Gavin fiddled with the small stack of books on his desk, realigning them with their spines facing a different direction. He tried to think about what he would take with him to Crowsmouth, but his thoughts drifted right back to his father and the hollowness settling into his chest.

"Owned by Duke Waldren, I take it?"

"Owned by the crown for quite some time, but originally, yes."

"I can see why your father fancies him a villain." Marcas turned and arched his brows, eyes sympathetic. "Gavin, it's not your fault he's changed."

"I should have seen the signs earlier. Years ago." Gavin shook his head and stood, moving to join Marcas at the window. At first, he focused on the grounds; then his focus shifted to their reflection, and his breath caught in his throat.

"Stop beating yourself up, love. If I would've seen the signs Rhona had slid off her rocker earlier...I still wouldn't have been able to do anything to stop it. I was too young. Too naïve. I wanted to believe she'd changed because she'd grown up, so I did. Until she began endangering my career and her own well-being." Marcas shook his head. "By then it was far too late. If anything could have been done to begin with."

"That's just it... You're right. It's not my fault he changed before, and it's not my fault now." Gavin leaned against Marcas and wrapped his arms around him, needing the contact, the security of his embrace. He let out an awkward laugh as Marcas held him and kissed his forehead. "I feel terrible that I'm relieved it's *not* my fault."

"Don't do that. You've done nothing but what he expected of you, even when it meant putting your life in danger. He can't recognise it anymore, but I can. Everyone around you can." Marcas lifted Gavin's chin and gazed into his eyes, his smile warm and full of love. "You're a good son."

Gavin's eyes welled with tears, but he smiled at his husband and leaned in for a much-needed kiss. Relief washed over him, quieting his doubts and fears. He might not ever hear those words from his father, but hearing them from the man he loved made all the difference.

THE END

ABOUT THE AUTHOR

Elliot Cooper is all about happy endings and positive queer rep in genre fiction - specifically subgenres of romance and erotica. His stories range from sweet to scorching hot, light to dark, humorous to serious, and everything in between. He loves to experiment with genre mash-ups and old favorite tropes, turning some on their heads, meeting others head-on.

Keep up to date on upcoming releases by signing up for Elliot's newsletter.

And please leave a review!

facebook.com/elliotcooperwrites

twitter.com/elliotwrites

ALSO BY ELLIOT COOPER

SWEET ROMANCE

The Clockwork Menagerie

Ace of Squids

Hearts Alight

ROMANCE

Stowaway

My Boyfriend's Back

Rogue Wolf

EROTIC ROMANCE & EROTICA

Stray Pup

Thirsty Boy

NON-ROMANCE

Working Stiffs

LIKE FREE BOOKS?

Follow the instructions at this link to get your free ebook:
www.elliotcooperwrites.com/vip-signup

CPSIA information can be obtained
at www.ICGtesting.com
Printed in the USA
LVHW112236290419
616043LV00001B/325/P